Protecting *Fate*

a Serve novel

Katee Robert

This book is a work of fiction. Names, characters, places, and incidents are the product of the author's imagination or are used fictitiously. Any resemblance to actual events, locales, or persons, living or dead, is coincidental.

Copyright © 2015 by Katee Robert. All rights reserved, including the right to reproduce, distribute, or transmit in any form or by any means. For information regarding subsidiary rights, please contact the Publisher.

Entangled Publishing, LLC
2614 South Timberline Road
Suite 109
Fort Collins, CO 80525
Visit our website at www.entangledpublishing.com.

Brazen is an imprint of Entangled Publishing, LLC. For more information on our titles, visit www.brazenbooks.com.

Edited by Heather Howland
Cover design by Heather Howland
Photography by Shutterstock

Manufactured in the United States of America

First Edition March 2015

To Hilary – for being my partner in crime for more years than I care to count.

Chapter One

"You're being overprotective and paranoid." Sara Reaver paced the sidewalk, ignoring the stares of the people waiting in line to enter Serve. She turned to face the street and made an effort to keep her voice down. Uncle Rodger wasn't a fan of ugly *womanly* emotions—unless it was calculated to serve a purpose. Right now, the only reason she was in danger of losing her temper was his being an overprotective ass. "If I was anyone else, you wouldn't be trying to force me out of the city."

He sighed. "Sara, I'm not trying to force you anywhere. I told you not to push Jesse Nord too hard, and you ignored that order."

"He was half a second away from telling the truth. He just needed the right motivation." And if he'd come clean about why he was really in that parking garage last month, her client, Mrs. Morris, wouldn't be facing jail time. The woman was more concerned about her reputation than the possibility of going to jail, though, so for the time being, the media shit storm was Sara's focus. The client wasn't always right, but it was her job to fix the problem.

"You miscalculated and pissed off some dangerous men in the process. It'll blow over, but you need to be out of sight until it does."

It was on the tip of her tongue to beg him not to do this. She wasn't young or stupid enough to think that no one would hurt her for pushing too hard, but exiling her to the country was over the top. "I don't have to leave the city. I'll just lay low for a little while."

"I'm not taking any chances." And then her uncle went and dropped the bomb she'd been dreading. "I already talked to Garrett about it. He's got a man who will keep you out of trouble until this all blows over."

Sara could actually see the trap closing in around her, and it seemed the harder she struggled, the more it suffocated her. "I can't believe you talked to Garrett before you talked to me." That hurt, like they were so sure that she'd be unreasonable that they had to join forces to get her to do what they wanted. She started digging through her purse for a cigarette before she remembered that she'd quit over a year ago.

That wasn't a good sign.

She rubbed the bridge of her nose. "You're treating me like a child, and I resent it."

"Then prove I don't have to." He didn't sound the least bit sorry. "I expect you to be packed and ready to go tomorrow morning." He paused. "Don't make this any more difficult than it has to be, Sara."

The only person it was difficult for was *her*. *He* didn't

have to leave the city. *He* wasn't worried about being targeted by a pissed off CEO with ties to unsavory people. No, Uncle Rodger could take care of himself.

If only he had half as much faith in her ability to do the same.

But it didn't matter that she was one of the best fixers he had on his team and had a knack for finding creative ways out of the situations that their clients came to them with.

Or that she could take out nearly everyone on both the shooting range and the practice mat. No, all that mattered was that she was little Sara Reaver, the niece he used to cart around on his shoulders—or whatever other memory he dragged up whenever it suited him. He was even worse than her brothers. The fact that he'd drawn them in—because when it came to family, anything Garrett knew, Will knew—was only the icing on the cake.

She was trapped and they both knew it.

As tempting as stomping her foot and digging in her heels sounded, it wouldn't make her uncle respect her more. In fact, it was all but guaranteed to make him put her in the equivalent of the time-out chair for months. So she forced herself to unclench her teeth. "I'll be ready."

"Good. Text me when you're on the road."

"Of course." She hung up and only barely resisted the urge to fling her phone into the street. She wanted to call her brother and lay into him, but that wouldn't do any good. And she couldn't call her best friend, Ridley, either, because she was most likely attached at the hip to Garrett. As happy as she was that they'd figured stuff out, it was damned inconvenient right now.

Her thumb traced the screen. She could call Will. He had

a wonderful habit of cutting to the heart of things without letting messy emotions get in the way. But that was before he'd gone and fallen in love. And gotten engaged. He might try to help, but no doubt he had better things to do with his night than listen to her bitch about something that was beyond both of their control.

Especially since things had been so *weird* since her brothers fell into love and relationships and engagements. She was happy for them. Truly, she was. But a part of her had always thought that the Reaver siblings would ride off into the sunset, single until the end of time. After all, they'd seen just how quickly marital bliss could turn into a nightmare that a person didn't simply walk away from.

They crawled, broken and bleeding.

That person you loved so much it consumed you could wake up one day, and be a stranger, everything you thought you knew about them suddenly a lie. If it could happen after twenty years of marriage, she didn't hold out much hope that anyone was safe. The only real law of life was change, and that proved double for people in relationships. She'd seen the horrible confusion and betrayal on her father's face, had heard him whisper the questions that had no real answers.

Why are you leaving? Why aren't you happy anymore? Why don't you love us enough to stay?

Sara really hoped her brothers' happiness would last, but she wasn't about to throw her hat into the ring with a guy and hope for the best.

Love couldn't hurt her if she didn't give it a chance.

With a sigh, she dropped her phone into her purse, doing her best to ignore the sliver of betrayal that always seemed to dig in when she thought about her brothers moving into the next stage of life.

Sara turned and faced Serve. If she had one night of freedom left, she might as well enjoy it. Normally, she avoided this place. Both her brothers frequented it with depressing regularity, and her therapy bill was already high enough without adding seeing a sibling in a sexual situation to the list. But if Garrett was busy arranging a babysitter for her, he wasn't here, and Will and Penelope had plans tonight of a non-kinky variety. The coast was as clear as it could possibly be.

That meant at least something good would come from this fiasco.

A little bounce worked its way into her step as she bypassed the line, gave the bouncer a quick peck on the cheek, and strode into another world. The owner of Serve, Jonah, was as hilarious as he was sexy. Newbies came in expecting NYC's premier BDSM club to be all dark and gothic and serious, but the reality was totally different. Everything was very tongue-in-cheek, from the DJs who favored Muse, to the giant mouth framing the elevator up to the actual BDSM portion of the club. It made Sara grin every time she saw it.

She didn't plan on wasting time with drinks tonight—if she only had one night, she intended to use it to the fullest. A little thrill went through her as she cut her way around the bar and grinned at the manager, Nolan. "Hey, handsome."

"Hey, yourself." He was gorgeous, like all the employees there seemed to be, his hair like the best dark red wine and his eyes a delicious deep brown. The difference between Nolan and everyone else was that Jonah trusted him enough to be in charge of the day-to-day operations. He kept asking her out, but she preferred to keep things on a Serve-only basis. "You going up?"

"That depends." She leaned into him, liking his muscles despite the fact that no sparks erupted in her stomach at the contact. It was better this way. Safer. "When are you off?"

"For you? Give me fifteen minutes to find a replacement."

She grinned. "Perfect."

...

Z watched Garrett's little sister flirt with the manager, the invitation clear in every line of her body. He'd never met her in person, but Garrett talked about her enough that he felt like he knew her. Sara Reaver, as troublesome as she was pretty. And she was pretty. Tonight she wore a short black dress that showed off her legs to perfection, but it was the pearls that really got him. Pearls were something he'd always associated with old women who had more money than sense. To see them on this little blonde who obviously had dirty plans on her mind?

Yeah, it did things for him.

Z set his drink aside as the elevator doors closed behind her. Garrett told him she was in trouble, and that she wasn't likely to agree to leave the city without a fight. Hard to say at this point, but she sure as hell looked like she planned to have fun tonight.

He should let her have it. The exit strategy officially came into play tomorrow, so what would it hurt to give the woman one last night of freedom?

But what if something happened because he'd decided to back off?

He found himself walking up to the elevator before he'd

finished the thought. She was more than a job—she was kin to one of the only men in this world he trusted, which meant he couldn't afford mistakes. Once he'd told Garrett where they were, the man had made a call and gotten him on the list to be allowed upstairs—with the understanding that he wouldn't interact with anyone beyond Sara.

That was fine. Z hadn't let himself off the leash in years, and he wasn't about to start the night that his friend's little sister was potentially in danger. He knew all too well how things went tits up when he lost control, after the last time...

He nodded at the manager and gave his name. The man raised his eyebrows, but stepped aside. "Jonah has specific rules for you. Don't break them." He paused, as if considering adding something, and it didn't take a genius to know he was considering warning Z off Sara.

Z waited, genuinely curious. For all that she'd been flirting and sending all the signals that this man would get lucky tonight, there hadn't been the genuine level of comfort that came along with a relationship. Beyond that, either Garrett or his uncle would know if Sara was actually seeing someone, and they'd agreed she wasn't. Z wasn't naive enough to think she'd share such information willingly, but both had their ways of finding that kind of thing out without her knowing.

Either way, she wasn't seeing *this* man.

He headed upstairs, pushing the button for the first upper floor since he wasn't sure where she'd be. Of the three upper floors, they were rated by degree of how hardcore the play was. He stepped onto the second upper floor and looked around the room. There was a spanking bench and a few other things set up for scenes, but the room was dominated by a large sitting area that seemed designed more for chatting than anything kink or sex related.

But no Sara.

He turned and took the elevator to the next floor. And there she was, lounging on a couch next to two men who seemed to be hanging on her every word. Not that he could blame them—even from across the room, there was something about her that drew him. He wanted to talk to her, to hear what her voice sounded like, to get a better look at the way the pearls draped over the curve of her breasts.

Z shook his head. What the fuck was he thinking? She was a body to protect, no matter how slight the risk might be, and that meant he had no business thinking about *her* body. He didn't make a habit of taking protection jobs—wouldn't have taken this one if it wasn't Garrett asking—but he'd never had a problem keeping things contained before. The fact that he hadn't even spoken to her and her presence was already pushing at his control wasn't a good sign.

Different scenes were in play around him, the sensory overload only setting him further on edge. *Keep it reined in, man. Get the girl, and get out of here.* Because he *wanted* to stop and watch the man whipping the woman bent over a bench, pausing every few strokes to finger her between her legs. Or the couple fucking on the couch across from Sara, in plain view of anyone who cared to watch. Or the Dom tying his sub to the bondage contraption, creating a fascinating pattern with purple rope across her body. It was like fucking Candyland in here.

Which meant he needed to leave. Now.

He stopped in front of her. "Sara Reaver."

She stared at his boots and took her time working up

to his eyes, a slow smile curving her lips. "Today's not my birthday, but I'm not about to complain."

"We need to talk."

"Baby, I'll kiss your boots and call you Daddy if it means you'll play with me." But then her blue gaze sharpened on his face and her smile fell away. "Wait a minute. I know you." She shot to her feet. "They said I had until tomorrow. Get the hell out of here."

It was tempting to do exactly that, because he couldn't help but see the way her breasts heaved with each breath, or notice she barely came up to his shoulder even with her heels, despite the fact her legs seemed three miles long in that short dress. "I can't do that."

"Can't, or won't?" She shook her head. "It doesn't matter. I'm not leaving."

That was what he was afraid of. Being here was a drug to his system, lulling him into the promise of what could be. He knew better. He'd learned the hard way, letting go had very real consequences that were impossible to contain. He'd made a promise to himself seven years ago, and he'd never had a problem with even being tempted to break it. Until now. Standing here, staring down at her, he was having a hell of a time remembering all the reasons he had to never go *there* again.

While he'd been lost in a furious inner battle, Sara seemed to have decided on something. She sidled closer, her lily perfume teasing him as she ran a single finger down his chest. "I have the perfect idea. Why don't *you* stay and play with me?" Her finger stopped just short of the top button of his jeans. "I want to see how closely you can guard my body."

Chapter Two

Sara was just messing with the man, because he couldn't show up here to ruin her last night of freedom and expect her to be on her best behavior. She'd worked long and hard to actually *have* a best behavior, so she'd be taken seriously, and she hadn't been able to let off any steam in longer than she cared to think about. Tonight had been important for that alone—especially since it was now her last hurrah before she was shipped off to God knew where.

Plus, she could see the first flickering of desire in those strange green eyes. If this guy worked with Garrett, then he was a master of control. She'd have to be a saint not to try to test him. While she'd been called many things in her life, a saint wasn't one of them. She tugged the waistband of his jeans, studying his face. He had model cheekbones, though there was something unfinished about his features. It kept him from being pretty, instead shoving him into ruggedly handsome territory. His plain white T-shirt set off his dark skin, another contrast, and she couldn't help checking out the scars scattered over his left arm. Where had he picked up those?

Then he stepped back, trying to put some distance between them. "It isn't like that."

"Why not?" She didn't *really* want to sleep with this guy. He was friends with her brother and, while that would have been enough to put him in forbidden fruit territory, she liked to think she'd outgrown such childish impulses. Mostly. But she followed him, backing him up another three steps before he seemed to realize he was retreating from a woman half his size.

His eyebrows slammed down over those pale eyes and he straightened, gaining another inch. He was easily as tall as her twin brothers—six-three, at least—and just as wide. The close-cropped haircut pegged him as former military, but she didn't need the visual clue to know that. It was in every tense muscle and the way he held himself as if ready to spring into motion at any moment. Plus, all of Garrett's team were former military of one flavor or another.

Sara ran her hands up his chest, silently delighting in how cut he was, and looped them around his neck, bringing them chest-to-chest. "I want you. You *obviously* want me." She pressed her hips against his, her breath catching in her throat when she found him rock hard. *Holy crap.*

Get a hold of yourself, Reaver. This is just a game.

Right.

"Enough." He took her wrists, holding her as if she was a poisonous snake, and stepped back again. "We need to talk."

Uptight, wasn't he? She glanced back to find the two Doms she'd been chatting up watching with avid interest.

It wouldn't do for them to think she was getting rejected. She liked her image of the untouchable sub who only let a select one or two play with her when the mood struck. If they thought this man was turning her down... Well, her pride wouldn't stand for it. She flicked the stranger's lower lip. "Fine. Have it your way. Follow me."

She turned and headed down the hallway to the private rooms. No doubt the man wanted to take her somewhere that wasn't Serve, but she wasn't ready to leave yet. She had a date set with Nolan, and since it was likely the only action she'd get in the foreseeable future, she wasn't about to miss it. It was blatantly obvious this guy wasn't going anywhere until they talked, and, as much as she loved the idea of an audience, having him glower at her while she was trying to get lucky was a serious downer.

There was only one open room, and she wasted no time claiming it. It was only when the door was shut and locked that the man seemed to relax a little. He prowled around the room, his dark skin gleaming in the low light. God, he looked good enough to eat. What was Garrett thinking, assigning such a tempting morsel to watch over her? Oh, right. That she was an adult who should know better. She sighed. Responsibility sucked sometimes, but Uncle Rodger wouldn't have agreed to take her on in the first place if he thought she'd let her impulses get the better of her.

And she hadn't. Until that bastard, Nord, had gotten busy with that prostitute in the parking garage while someone who was *not* her client had been breaking into a nearby car to steal some files containing delicate information. Everyone around knew Nord was a tough son of a bitch, but she'd been so focused on getting her client cleared, she hadn't stopped to consider that he might not like her putting his marriage in jeopardy.

In short, she might have been a little naïve there.

Sara dropped onto the bed, well aware how closely the guy watched her, and patted the mattress next to her. "Why don't you sit and we can get down to business." His glare was unrelenting, and he took the chair across from the bed. She huffed, even though she really hadn't expected him to sit on the bed. "God, you're already a pain in my ass and it's been a grand total of five minutes."

"Your brother mentioned that you're difficult."

That was a classic case of the pot calling the kettle black. She was no more difficult than any of the Reaver siblings—even if they didn't see things that way. But she was supposed to be taking this seriously, so she made an effort to stop eyeballing the impressive bulge in the front of his jeans. "How about we start with introductions. I'm Sara. You are?"

"I know who you are." When she just waited, he sighed. "I'm Z."

Z? *The* Z? The godlike leader of Garrett's squad, who could do no wrong? She sat up straighter. From what she understood, he was typically off leading missions that were on the far side of dangerous, in parts of the world most people had never heard of. While their company did take bodyguard missions from time to time—and Garrett *loved* to bitch about them—Z seemed to delegate those. "Why didn't you send one of your men instead?"

"I have my reasons."

Meaning she'd have to dig to find them out. Interesting. At least it would give her something to do while she was in exile—otherwise she was bound to die of boredom. She leaned forward, noting the way his gaze followed the movement. "You wanted to talk?"

"We need to go over the security measures I have in place." He looked around the room, some unidentifiable expression on his face. "This isn't where I wanted to have the conversation."

This isn't really where she wanted to have this conversation, either. "Tough shit. My uncle told me to be ready tomorrow morning, and I will be. He didn't say anything about tonight."

"Your need for protection doesn't start in the morning."

It was an effort not to throw her hands up in frustration. She'd done her research on Nord before she approached him—she wasn't a complete idiot—and he had nothing in his history that indicated he liked to make people disappear. While it was possible he was just that good, she had a hard time giving him so much credit. It was far more likely the man was just spouting bullshit in hopes that she'd get scared and back off. She *hated* giving him what he wanted, even though she had no choice in the matter. "I don't need protection at all. My uncle is overreacting."

"All the same." That was it. As if the matter were already decided.

Which it was, no matter how intensely she disliked the outcome. She could either take it gracefully, or she could throw a tantrum and prove them all right in their belief that she was still a little girl in need of protection. Sara lifted her chin. She sure as hell wasn't going to do the latter.

Her phone chimed, and she glanced down to find a text from Nolan. *We still on?* She typed out a quick affirmation, shooting a look at Z from the corner of her eye. Nolan wasn't the insecure type, so *he* must have said something to make the man doubt she still wanted a scene. Apparently nothing was going to go right tonight. Right now, she should be naked and in the middle of some really awesome sex—not talking to this man who was as pissy as he was sexy. There was something about Z that made her want to poke at him, to see how good his control really was.

Since he was there, effectively ruining her night, and providing a really attractive target for all her frustration and anger, it was only fair that she returned the favor. Just a little. She kicked off her heels and slid off the mattress, walking around the bed to the chest situated at the end. Best-case scenario, he got wigged out and left her to Nolan. Worst case... Well, she'd just have to make sure this ended in a best-case scenario.

"What are you doing?"

"You're interrupting my fun. So while you talk, I'm getting ready." She glanced over her shoulder, finding his gaze glued on her ass. Something fluttered low in her stomach at the intensity of that look, but she ignored it. She was supposed to be making *him* uncomfortable. "So, talk."

Z cleared his throat. "There will be three men on duty—myself in the house with you, and two others set up to watch from a distance."

"Kinky." She found the cuffs she was looking for and tossed them onto the bed. A second set followed.

"Your uncle picked the location, and we'll drive out there tomorrow."

Sara hooked two cuffs to the bottom of the bed frame and moved around to hook the remaining two to the top. "So the four of us are going on a little road trip. Lovely."

"You won't have contact with my men."

She glanced at him in surprise. "Why not?"

"I have my reasons."

He sounded so uptight, it was enough to make her wonder if he'd shatter into a million pieces if she poked too hard. She wasn't exactly an expert at bodyguard stuff, but it seemed strange how he was setting things up. "Afraid I'll corrupt them?"

"No." Just that. Nothing else.

Another glance at him found him just as stiff and unyielding as before. There was no reason for her to expect any different. Really, a small, stupid part of her found his distance kind of hot—a part she had *no* intention of letting take the reins. She would keep her head down and get through this just like she'd gotten through everything in her life up to that point. The so-called danger would pass and things would get back to normal. It was as simple as that.

But that did nothing to change how things would play out tonight. She needed the release Nolan was sure to provide, if she was going to be able to handle being out of the city for…however long it took for Uncle Rodger to calm things down. Which meant Z had to leave. Now. "Great. Sounds like a plan. I'll see you in the morning." When he didn't move, she realized she was going to have to take extreme measures. With a mental shrug, Sara reached for the strap of her dress.

• • •

Z was sure she was bluffing right up until the moment the dress hit the floor. He went stock-still, helpless to look away from her body, from the panties that covered a laughably small amount, to the pearls that dripped down between her breasts, framing them more than covering them. Her nipples were the same color as her lips, a rosy pink that drew his attention and threatened to make him forget all the reasons he couldn't touch her.

For her part, Sara didn't seem that concerned with being mostly naked in a room with a man she'd just met. She crawled onto the bed, the move giving him an excellent view of her round ass, and then propped up the pillows against the headboard. She cuffed first one ankle, and then the other, leaving her legs splayed open.

Fuck.

He cleared his throat, but it did nothing to diminish the growing monster in his chest. Images flashed behind his eyes—of moving over her while she was spread eagle and helpless to do anything but take whatever he chose to give her, of ripping those panties off to bare her completely, of putting her over his knee and... He shut that shit down. *No.* He *refused* to go there again. "What are you doing?"

"I have a date in ten minutes." She reached for the cuff on one side of her head and frowned.

Against his better reason, Z stood and moved closer to the bed. "And this is how you start your dates?"

"Don't take that Puritan tone with me. You're in Serve. What did you think people do here—bake cookies and tell bedtime stories?" She laughed. "The only stories we tell are the kinky hot ones."

He knew that. Of course he knew that. But knowing that and seeing his best friend's little sister mostly naked and tied to a bed were two different things. He had no business thinking dark thoughts about her, or wondering how she'd taste, or if she'd purr his name in that husky voice when he pushed his cock inside her. Z shook his head, wishing he could shake loose the thoughts so easily. But once they began, they rooted down deep, and he knew from past experience that they'd rise again at the least opportune moment.

"What do you know about this man?" He mentally cursed himself as soon as the words came out of his mouth. Protection or not, he'd just met the woman and had no business prodding at her sex life.

She raised her eyebrows. "Well, I just pulled him off the street because I liked his muscles. Why? Do you think that's a bad idea?" She snorted. "I wish you could see the look on your face right now."

He tried to rein himself in. "It's not my business."

"You're right. It's not. Now, can you help me fasten this last cuff?" She waved her remaining free wrist at him.

Z surveyed the bed, but it was shoved up against the wall, so there was no way he could get within reach of the cuff without climbing up onto the mattress with her. It was unprofessional in the extreme, and a terrible idea in the mix, but he found himself doing just that. She was temptation personified, lying on the bed, her pale body framed by red sheets, her golden hair a tangle around her, her legs spread in open invitation.

Not an invitation for me. He had to remember that. She was a body to guard, not a woman he could touch. But Z found himself running his hand from her shoulder to her wrist, marveling at how soft her skin was, and then reached for the cuff. He closed the Velcro around her and tugged on it. "Too tight?"

"Just right." A flush spread across her chest, and she seemed to be breathing a little faster.

He should get off the bed and move away. He knew it. But instead he sat onto the mattress next to her, letting himself look his full. "He's a lucky man."

"That goes without saying." She watched his face, frowning as if she couldn't quite work something out. "I have a question for you, Z."

He dropped his gaze to the scrap of cloth covering the dip between her thighs. He could *swear* it was damp from her desire. His control fractured a little more. "What?"

"Do you want me?" Her voice seduced him as thoroughly as the sight of her body. "I can feel your eyes on me. Do you want to touch me?"

Yes. Fuck, yes. He was actually reaching out to do just that when he caught himself. What the fuck was he doing? Not only was she his charge, but she was Garrett's little sister. He should have put a stop to this the second she took off her clothes instead of letting her coax him closer, until he was actually considering taking her up on the offer that blazed from her eyes. Z snatched his hand back and pushed off the bed so fast, it was only his quick reflexes that kept him from tripping.

Those blue eyes gave no mercy. "Maybe you're more of a watcher. Would you like to sit there on that chair and watch me touch myself?"

Yes. He gritted his teeth. "No."

"Liar."

It dawned on him that this woman was trained by the same man who trained Garrett. She could read his interest, even as he tried to hide it. Shit. Z turned away, closing his eyes, but it did no good. The sight of a half-naked Sara Reaver would be imprinted in his mind from now until kingdom come.

"You need to be protected," he said.

"You're more than welcome to stay." He could hear the smile in her voice. "I like an audience."

He couldn't be sure of his reactions if he did stay. He had no claim on this woman, but the thought of sitting and watching another man touch her... Z couldn't do it. So he walked to the door, keeping his back to her. "I'll be at your apartment tomorrow at seven. Be ready."

Then he fled. There was no other word for it. He could comfort himself with calling it a tactical retreat, but the truth was he hustled out of there as if there were hounds of hell on his heels.

Chapter Three

Sara huffed out a breath. She'd only meant to poke at Z, but the sheer *want* in his eyes when he looked at her had been unexpected, to say the least. And she'd responded. *Of course* she'd responded—she'd have to be dead not to. The man was tempting in a way she never would have expected from hearing stories about him. He'd looked at her like he was the big bad wolf, and if she made a wrong move, he'd be only too happy to gobble her up.

There had been men who'd wanted her—she was attractive enough that she never had to worry about her dance card being empty—but it was like the difference between a puppy and a junkyard dog. If she had half a brain in her head, she'd chalk this up to temporary insanity and pretend it never happened.

She dropped back onto the pillows and sighed. Obviously it had been too much to ask for a night of hot sex with no strings attached before she was shipped off. She and Nolan weren't anywhere near her three date/fuck limit, but now she couldn't dredge up any of the interest she'd felt before she came upstairs. Damn Z for leaving her like this, all cold and hot and twisted up.

Because, even knowing it was a horrible idea, she wanted him more than she had any right to.

It didn't make any sense. Sara might like playing on the wild side from time to time, but she wasn't stupid. Sleeping with her bodyguard—who happened to be her older brother's best friend—was a recipe for disaster. It was something she might have tried when she was nineteen and still in the middle of her wild and crazy days. Now? Now, she knew better.

Or she was *supposed* to.

The door opened, and her entire body went tight with anticipation…right up until Nolan walked into the room. Damn it. She'd been *excited* about Nolan, had been ready to rock his world seven ways to Sunday.

But one talk with Z had gone and ruined everything. She tried and failed to dredge up a smile. The whole night was one big mark in the loss column. At this point, she might as well go home, pour herself a glass of wine, and try to get some sleep. "Hey, handsome. Can you untie me? I'm going to have to take a rain check on our play date."

He was at her side in an instant, brown eyes concerned. "Are you okay? Did someone step out of line?" It was clear from his tone that he had one particular person in mind.

"No, I'm fine." Or she would be as soon as she exorcised Z from her realm of possibilities. She didn't believe in that fairy tale connection, but she was a big fan of lust at first sight. This felt different, though. Sara wasn't sure what the hell it was, but she didn't like it. *So forget it. That's the best way to move forward.*

Easier said than done.

Since she couldn't promise her full attention to Nolan, she wasn't about to burn one of the three times with him tonight. So she smiled, climbed off the bed, and pulled on her dress. "Really, I'm fine."

"I'd believe it more if you didn't have *that* look in your eyes."

"What look?" She tried for innocence, but Nolan wasn't stupid. He had a knack for seeing things she'd rather not share.

Like now. "Like you got your toes trampled all over."

Considering that was exactly how she felt, she didn't have much she could say in response. But Sara patted his cheek and kept her smile bright. "Not by you. That's all you need to worry about."

"Sara—"

God save her from overprotective men. "I'm fine. Really. I just need to get some sleep." She slipped out of the room before Nolan could call her on her lie. Not that he would have, even if she'd stayed. They were casual at best, and while he might be a good man, he had no claim on her. There was only so far he could push, and they both damn well knew it.

Which was exactly how she liked things. Sara had enough overprotective men in her life without adding another—especially one she just wanted to have hot, wall-banging sex with.

Or, God forbid, one who worked with her brother.

She headed out to the street, ignoring the party in full swing down on the club level. On another night, she'd be right there in the midst of it, dancing and drinking and having the time of her life. Tonight, it held no more appeal than the upper floors did. Damn Z to hell and back.

The cab ride back to her apartment went by entirely too fast. She still hadn't managed to center herself by the time she stepped out onto the sidewalk. The cold night air did nothing to cool the heat pulsing from her skin. It was all too easy—too tempting—to close her eyes and picture *his* pale green eyes tracking her every movement. She'd played sub before, when the opportunity arose, but Sara had never felt quite so...hunted. She might have been able to push through on sheer bravado because she'd surprised him, but she didn't like her chances of being successful a second time.

Which is why there couldn't be a second time.

Z had all the hallmarks of a man who wouldn't allow himself to be topped from the bottom. It might be her imagination getting the best of her, but he struck her as the type to demand *everything*. And everything was too high a cost, even for someone who made her react with just a look.

Then why are you still thinking about him? Take a deep breath, and get your head on straight because you're going to be spending a whole hell of a lot of time with him in the near future.

She'd dealt with difficult men—and women—in the past. She could do this. The alternative... There wasn't one. He wouldn't touch her, even if she wanted it. His training was too ingrained and the man wore his control like a suit of armor. So if she didn't get a hold of herself, she'd be panting after him like... Well, like something that wasn't attractive in the least. She was better than that. She had to be.

Sara pushed through the door and into the relative heat

of her building. It was entirely possible that this exile was a test to see how well she followed orders. Uncle Rodger wasn't above doing something like that, though she'd thought she'd moved past that kind of thing years ago. Either way, she couldn't risk screwing this up.

"Being a responsible adult is overrated." She unlocked her apartment door and frowned when it didn't immediately swing open. She pushed it, encountered resistance again, and pushed harder. It gave with a groan, opening another few inches.

Enough to see that her living room had been trashed.

Every instinct demanded she rush in there and look for the few mementos she actually cared about, but her training kicked in. She took two steps back, cursed, and nearly ran from the building. There was a little corner store halfway down the block that was open at all hours, and that was where she ducked through the front door. Sara dialed her uncle with shaking fingers.

"Hello?" Despite the late hour, he sounded as sharp as ever.

"I have a problem."

"Where are you?"

"Not my apartment." She took a deep breath, fighting for calm. "It's been tossed." She gave him the rundown with what little detail she had, and her current location.

"Stay where you are. I'm sending someone over."

"Okay." Sara hung up, her stomach sinking when she realized exactly *whom* he was sending over. Shit.

...

Z didn't break into a run simply because it would draw attention. If whoever went through Sara's apartment was watching, he didn't need them knowing he was attached to their target. *Target*. His skin crawled at the wrongness of that term being associated with the little blonde who was so full of life. She had to be protected.

He cut across the street and ducked into the store Rodger said she'd be in. At first glance, it was empty, but he walked down the main aisle and caught sight of her, huddled and staring at the display in front of her. She spoke when he stopped a few feet away from her, "You know, I've been here ten minutes and I still can't decide. What do you think? Should I go ultra-ribbed for her pleasure, or with the magical sensations of hot and cold?"

"What?" He followed her gaze and frowned. "Why are you looking at condoms?" More than that, why was she here instead of in the middle of losing herself with Serve's manager? He couldn't ask that, though. He had no right to the information, and the fact that he was pleased she'd cancelled was completely out of line.

"I can only spend so long staring at chips and Gatorade. At least condoms have entertainment value." She shrugged and finally turned to face him. "So what's the plan?"

"Getting you out of here." When she didn't move, he motioned toward the front door. "The sooner, the better."

"No."

Z frowned. "Yes." He actually went so far as to reach for her before he realized what he was doing and aborted the movement.

But she was already shaking her head. "I have stuff in my apartment that I need."

"Buy new."

"I don't know about you, but I'm not made of money." She crossed her arms over her chest. "And some things are irreplaceable."

Now wasn't the time to tell her that her uncle had given him damn near an unlimited budget to keep her happy. Or that Z was more than capable of replacing anything she had in her apartment twice over out of his own funds. He had to get her out of here by whatever means necessary—get her *safe*. "Make a list." When she still didn't move, he ground his teeth.

"Is this where you tell me that we can do this the easy way or the hard way?"

"No." He pulled her toward him and bent down, tossing her over his shoulder in a smooth movement. She cursed, but he had a job and that job wouldn't be changed for difficult women. Z nodded to the shell-shocked cashier as he stepped out onto the street and headed for the town car he'd rented. A quick check in the front showed one of his men, Joe. He set Sara into the backseat as carefully as he could and then climbed in behind her.

Right in time to catch a right hook to the jaw.

He reeled back, but that didn't keep him from stopping her next punch, encasing her fist with his hand. "Enough."

"You can't just throw me over your shoulder whenever you think I'm being too difficult. There's this neat little thing called words—normal people use them before skipping straight to force."

"I used words. Words which you ignored."

"Then use better words."

"Sara." He waited for her to stop huffing and meet his

gaze. "You were getting in this car one way or another, and we both know it."

"Ass," she hissed. "Both you and my uncle."

"Maybe." His job was to keep her safe, and sometimes doing so meant keeping his charges safe from themselves. It was entirely possible that whoever trashed her apartment was long gone, but hoping for that wasn't worth the risk of allowing her back there. She knew it—or she would as soon as she calmed down and thought things through.

But he wasn't going to be her personal punching bag in the meantime.

Z looked up in time to see her shifting. He squeezed her fist, hard enough to show her he meant business. "You were entitled to one hit. Any more and there will be consequences."

"What, are you going to hit me back?"

Did she realize she got damn near belligerent when she was frightened? He'd seen it in men back during his days in the Army. They got scared and immediately picked a fight with someone bigger, just to prove they weren't. He didn't find it any more endearing with Sara than he had with them. "I don't hit women." Before she could look too smug, he continued. "But I will not hesitate to put you over my lap and spank you until you beg for mercy."

Her blue eyes went wide. "Oh."

He couldn't believe he'd given those dark desires voice. Or his reaction to doing so. It was all too easy to picture doing just that to her—yanking up her dress to bare her from the waist down and using his hand to redden her ass. *Fuck*. Z had no more success banishing that image than he had back at Serve, so he tried to focus on the immediate problem.

Satisfied she wouldn't try to hit him again, he let go of

her fist and sat back. "Text your uncle the items you want and my man will bring them out in the morning." He watched her type away at her phone, satisfied she was obeying. For once. When she pushed send, he noted that her hands were shaking. Shit. Her attitude was one thing—he'd dealt with that kind of thing before—but this was something else. Z specialized in putting himself and his team into some of the most dangerous situations known to man, but put him in a car with a shaking woman and he was at a loss.

What was he supposed to do? Pull her into his arms and hold her until she stopped? The idea was more attractive than it should be, which meant that was exactly what he *shouldn't* do. But he still found himself reaching for her.

Sara looked up at him. "I have a question."

"Ask." He laid his arm over the back of the seat to cover his intention. Fuck, this was worse than being in high school and trying to figure out if making the first move would get him a kiss or a slap. He wasn't made for comfort. He never had been.

She leaned back, her long hair brushing against his forearm. "Would you really put me over your knee if I hit you again?"

He went rock hard at the thought. Because there wasn't fear, or even intimidation, in her tone. No, she sounded both curious and turned on. He cleared his throat and lied, "No."

"Liar." She put her hand on his thigh, entirely too close to his cock. "I think you'd love to do exactly that, to yank up my dress while I struggle, and spank me until my skin goes red and I'm begging." And then the little troublemaker palmed him between his legs. "No need to saying anything— I have my answer right here."

Chapter Four

Sara saw the desire on Z's face, as clear as day. She *knew* she should sit back and start thinking about what the next step was, but she couldn't stop shaking and the heat coming off his body was the best thing she'd felt all day. So she scooted closer, until they were pressed together from knee to chest, her hand still on his cock. Maybe if he'd just touch her, she'd stop thinking about strangers in her apartment, violating one of her few safe places, touching her things. Her skin crawled at the thought.

So she kept going, needing to purge away the ugliness with something clean. "I think it took everything you had not to touch me back at Serve. To slip your hand between my legs and—"

He kissed her, his tongue slipping between her lips as if to put her words to rest. Well, if this was how he went about shutting her up, she was going to run her mouth more often. Sara shifted her grip on his cock, sliding her hand up and down the denim, squeezing until his arms came around her and he shifted her to straddle him. She had the presence of mind to glance over her shoulder at the glass dividing the backseat from the front, but he gripped her hair and brought her mouth back around to him. "He can't see or hear."

"Okay." She wouldn't really care if he *could* at this point, as long as Z didn't stop touching her.

He took her mouth again, and she sank into the kiss, losing herself in the feeling of his tongue stroking hers and his big hands palming her ass, urging her to ride him through their clothes. She reached for his belt, needing to follow through on the pressure building in her, demanding release, but he bracketed her wrists behind her with one hand while keeping the other tangled in her hair. "No." Her breath sobbed out before she could stop it, and Z's grip only tightened. He kissed down her throat. "You want this?"

"*Yes.*"

"Then relinquish control."

She was already shaking her head, but she didn't know if it was in protest or agreement. She arched her back, the position offering up her breasts for him, but his mouth stopped at her sternum. "Give it up, Sara." His voice had dropped a full octave and sounded more like a growl than a whisper.

She had the sudden hysterical thought that the man between her legs was more dangerous than any out for her blood in NYC. And he wanted her submission. "How long?"

His dark chuckle against her skin sent a line of lightning straight to her core. "Until I'm done with you."

Who was this man? Because he wasn't the same one who'd walked away from her in Serve, or even the one who'd thrown her over his shoulder less than half an hour ago. And, damn her to hell and back, she wanted him even more knowing that. He really was the big, bad wolf, and she wanted him to follow through on the promise of his grip on her body and his lips moving against her skin.

But did she want him enough to throw caution to the wind and take what he was offering?

Sara never went into any situation without first ensuring that she'd have the upper hand—especially sex. She definitely wasn't going to start now, no matter how much she wanted him. "Three."

"Three?"

"You get me three times. Then it ends."

Z made that growling sound again. "Fine." He lifted his head and met her eyes. "Pick a safe word, Sara."

Holy shit. She'd wondered if the spanking thing was an indication of darker desires. Apparently the answer was a resounding *yes*. She searched for a safe word. Normally, the few times she played, she stuck with the generic "red." It didn't feel right this time, for reasons she refused to examine too closely. Instead, she responded to the borderline feral look in his pale green eyes. "Wolfman." His slow grin did nothing but reinforce the similarities.

"We'll talk hard limits later."

Her head practically spun at how fast this had gone from zero to completely out of control. What was she thinking? She was going to be spending nearly every waking hour with this man for God knew how long. Sleeping with him—*submitting* to him—was the worst idea in a history of some truly terrible ideas.

But she couldn't have stopped if she wanted to. "Okay."

"Put your hands against the glass." He skirted his now

free hand up the inside of her thigh as she obeyed, and slipped a finger beneath her panties. "You're wet, sweetheart. Warm and wet and welcoming." He pushed into her, seeming to test her, and she nearly bit through her lip at the feeling of his thick finger inside her. Z let go of her hair and pushed her dress to the side, baring first one breast and then the other. "I like you in pearls."

"Make me come, and next time the only thing I'll wear is pearls."

He stopped the delicious stroking of his finger and glared. "Did I give you permission to speak?" When she opened her mouth, he cut her off before she got an answer out. "The only words I want to hear are 'Yes, Sir' or 'No, Sir.'"

It was an effort to swallow. "Yes, Sir."

"You will not speak unless spoken to." He pinched her nipple hard enough to make her cry out. "Understand?"

The backseat seemed to have jumped ten degrees hotter. "Yes, Sir."

"Please me, and I'll fuck you tonight until you lose track of how many times you come."

Big words, but she had the slightly horrified thought that he could actually follow through on his threat. It was becoming more and more apparent that she'd bit off more than she could chew with this man.

He pulled her panties to the side, and frowned. Before she could ask what the problem was—which would be a problem in and of itself since she wasn't supposed to speak—he shoved her dress up her body and over her head to wrap around her forearms. One good rip and her panties were gone, leaving her in only the pearls. Z's eyes slid half shut as he palmed her breasts. "You're beautiful, sweetheart.

But you already knew that."

His hands slid down her sides, his thumbs playing over each rib, to her hips. "You crave the harsh hand of control, don't you?" He glanced up, killing her protest before it reached her lips. "I have rules."

More talking? For a man of few words, he sure had a lot to say once he got going. Even worse, each harsh word stoked her desire higher. She closed her eyes, but they flew open when he pinched her thigh. Z glared. "Pay attention. You will not speak unless I give permission. You will also not come without my say so. Disobey and you will be punished." He parted her with two fingers, playing with her, circling close enough to brush her clit, but nowhere near close enough to push her over the edge. "If you touch yourself without my presence, you will be punished more severely. Do you understand?"

"Yes, Sir." She couldn't help rolling her hips, trying to guide him inside her.

"Good. Then we can begin."

...

Z knew this was wrong. He knew he should stop. He also knew he wasn't going to. That first touch of her lips against his had loosed his beast and there was no going back now. He sat back, still fingering her, and let himself look his fill. In the dark of the backseat, she was little more than a pale shadow, but an exquisite one all the same. He'd allowed her to set the limit of three times, but Z could be a patient predator, and he had no intention of being cut off from her before he'd taken his fill.

A small voice in the back of his head screamed that he was making a mistake from which there was no coming back, that once he had a taste of this, he wouldn't be able to stand losing it—not again—but he ignored it.

Already, she was unbelievably wet, obeying his every command without question. Power coursed through his body, making him feel as if he'd just downed a bottle of Jack.

It was tempting to undo his pants and replace his fingers with his cock. Too tempting. He took his fingers back, not touching her except where she straddled him. "Let's see how obedient you can be. Hold this position."

It was nearly as torturous for him as it had to be for her. He wanted to touch her, to taste her, to fuck her, more than he'd wanted anything in damn near seven years. It was like waking up from a dream and realizing that he was seated at a banquet in his honor and all he had to do was reach out to be privy to the greatest pleasures known to mankind. But reaching out meant breaking damn near every rule he'd put in place to keep himself in check.

Breaking those rules meant possibly putting Sara's life in danger.

That sobered him up—but only a little. His phone ringing brought him even further back. He put a finger to Sara's lips. "Not a word." Satisfied she was going to obey, he answered, "Loreto."

"You got her out okay?"

There was something wrong about talking to Garrett while the man's little sister was naked and splayed over his lap, but Z couldn't bring himself to move her. "We're halfway to the house now."

"Good. Her apartment looks like someone was trying to

prove a point. Nothing taken as far as I can tell, but they did a lot of damage."

"Hold on." He put the phone to his shoulder. "You wanted something from your apartment. What?"

She bit her lip, obviously torn between keeping that information to herself and the desire to actually get what she wanted. He waited for her to realize she didn't have a choice in answering, and the frustration on her face was a delight to behold. "A photo album under my mattress."

He waited, but there was nothing else forthcoming so he put the phone back to his ear. "Under the mattress there's a photo album. Your sister wants it."

"Let me see." There was grunting and cursing and then Garrett was back. "Sara always was a smart cookie. She cut a hole in the box frame and patched it back up. It's still here." She must have heard, because she relaxed, just a bit.

"We'll need that."

"Ridley and I'll bring it. She's about ready to rip my head off for not telling her that we were shipping Sara out of town, so it'll make her happy to know we're not fucking kidnappers." He muttered something that sounded like 'again.'

That depended on whom they asked. Sara had made it more than clear that she didn't want to leave NYC, and was only doing so under protest. He'd thought this job would be drudgery of the highest order, but it was shaping up to be more trouble than he could have anticipated—and all of it originated with the woman in his lap. She was a temptation he'd never expected and couldn't resist. "Good. Update me if you find anything else."

"Will do." Garrett hesitated. "Z, take care of her, man. She's my baby sister."

The reminder was like cold water thrown in his face. What the fuck was he doing, playing with Sara Reaver? He owed Garrett his life several times over, and he couldn't even keep his hands off the man's sister twelve hours after meeting her. He was exactly what his ex-wife, Jennifer, had accused him of being—a disgusting monster. He cleared his throat. "I will."

Sara watched him from her bent back position, her eyes catching the occasional headlight from the cars behind them. She was so damn beautiful, he almost threw caution to the wind for the second fucking time, but Garrett's voice in his head was too much. Z pulled her dress back down, clenching his teeth to resist kissing her breasts, and covered her. Then he lifted her into the seat next to him and crossed his arms over his chest.

He could actually feel her questions in the silence between them, her demands to know what the hell was wrong with him, even though she didn't say a word. "Give me your phone." He waited for her to obey, and then quickly popped out the battery and SIM card. Then he passed back a prepaid that he'd bought earlier that day. "I doubt they'll bother to track it, but we can't risk it. My number is programmed in the contacts."

She slipped it into her purse and turned to stare out the window. The minutes passed, ticking up to half an hour and then a full hour, and still she didn't say a word.

It was only when he looked over and found her asleep that he realized what she'd been doing. Obeying. The thought left him cold. How the fuck was he supposed to keep control of himself when she was so damn tempting and *obedient?*

Z slouched back against his seat and cursed long and low. It was going to be a hell of a long mission.

Chapter Five

Sara woke up as the car pulled to a stop. Her body still ached with unresolved pleasure, and combined with the short nap, it did nothing for her mood. She rubbed her hands over her arms, all too aware that she'd stupidly skipped a coat, since she hadn't planned on being outside much. Apparently Z didn't believe in turning on the heat—unless it was the sexual heat.

She opened the door and stepped out onto the driveway, determined to put him out of her mind despite his proximity. She had been guilty of running hot and cold in the past, but that man was in a completely different league. How the hell did he go from barely exchanging two words to her, to über Dom, and then back to treating her like she'd just crawled into his lap and tried to fuck him against his will?

Really, she should thank him for stopping before something happened that they couldn't take back. Her life was complicated enough without adding a man who affected her on a level unlike anyone in the past. Even now, she could feel his gaze on the back of her neck, hotter than fire and twice as dangerous.

She moved toward the house, only to be stopped by a hand on her arm. It was aggravating as all get out that she already knew who was touching her without looking back. She opened her mouth to tell him to keep his hands to himself, but the words wouldn't come. Sara cursed herself for following an order when she had no intention of submitting to him.

But she still couldn't make herself speak.

"Let Joe check it."

A small, dark man slipped out of the driver's door, very pointedly not looking at her, and disappeared through the front door. Sara jerked away from Z while they waited, gripping her own wrist hard enough to hurt, until she was able to force out, "Don't touch me again."

She turned to find him watching her with an unreadable expression on his face. "I'll do my best."

Was that supposed to be comforting? It didn't help that she wasn't sure what answer she was looking for. She didn't make a habit of being indecisive, but this man seemed to bring it out in her. One second she was deciding to seduce him, the next she was submitting, the next she didn't want him to touch her at all. It was enough to give her whiplash. She still wasn't sure if she should smack her brother or thank him for inadvertently putting a stop to her and Z's hookup in the backseat.

Maybe she'd do both.

Joe appeared in the front door and nodded. That was all Z needed to usher her into the house, his hand brushing the small of her back. She shot him a dark look that he returned with interest, reminding her again that this wasn't a man she could intimidate or manipulate.

That was fine. She liked a challenge. The only question was what outcome she wanted—for him to stay away from her, or lose control like he had earlier? Sara sighed. She'd figure it out later. Right now she wanted a bed and eight hours of sleep. Things would look different in the morning—less confusing, less dangerous.

Tomorrow, she'd get her photo album back and come up with some sort of plan.

"Where's my room?" She eyeballed the massive foyer. Had Uncle Rodger rented her a damn B and B? In the driveway, she'd been paying more attention to Z than the house, but being inside it made her think she'd missed a whole hell of a lot. The curving staircase led upward, looking like something Scarlett O'Hara would be comfortable on, and she could see a sitting room through one of the arched openings on the ground floor.

"Pick one in the west wing."

Apparently her uncle felt horrible about exiling her, because there was no other explanation for this place. She'd fully expected to be dropped off at some little one-room cabin with no Internet or hot water, and instead she got a house with *wings*. "I'm not exactly a Boy Scout, so am I going left or right at the top of the stairs?"

She thought she heard Z sigh. "Left."

"Great. Thanks." She forced herself to climb the stairs slowly instead of taking them two at a time, because she didn't want him to think she was running from him—even if that's exactly what it felt like. It was only when she was out of sight that she released the pent up breath she'd been holding. *Four hours down. God knows how many to go.* At least in a house this size, she could avoid him, if she ended up deciding that was what she wanted.

Sara peeked into rooms as she passed, each seeming to be their own suite, and finally settled on one halfway down the hall. It was green and generic enough to be for either a man or a woman, but what drew her were the huge windows dominating the wall across from the door. She flipped on the light and crossed to look out, and laughed.

"Yeah, Uncle Rodger is definitely trying to apologize." The house was U-shaped, and in the empty space between the wings, there was a pool encased in a glass greenhouse looking building. She loved swimming—had since she was a kid—and she'd just been bitching to him a few weeks ago about how all the hours she was putting in were making it impossible to make time for her laps. She grinned. Guess he'd been listening.

A light came on almost directly across from her, and her grin widened as she saw Z prowling around the room. He stopped in the window, and she could almost feel his glare as he faced her. Sara shook her head and closed the curtains. Let him stew a bit longer.

She stopped in front of the bed. She was exhausted, but the siren call of the pool was too much to resist. "A few laps and then I'll be tired enough to sleep." Simple. Right.

As if anything in her life was simple anymore.

...

Z's phone rang while he was still glaring at the closed curtains of Sara's room. She'd shut him out, which was no more than he deserved. But he resented the barrier between them all the same. With a curse, he answered his phone. "Loreto."

"Z?"

His entire body jumped to attention at Sara's husky voice on the other end. "Yeah."

"I have a question."

He primed himself to tell her that no, they couldn't fuck until they forgot both their names, because it was a shitty idea—and out of respect for her brother. He was so focused on composing his answer, he missed the question. "Say again?"

"That Joe guy. Where is he now?"

"Watching the road. My other guy, Logan, is covering the back half of the property."

"So no one close?"

Why the fuck was she asking this? "Just me. But there's no reason to worry—we'll know about any threat long before it gets close enough to actually be a problem."

"Sure." She hung up, leaving him staring out his window and wondering what the fuck just happened. He was in the process of dialing her back when movement below caught his eye. Sara stepped out into the lit pool area and pulled her dress off in a smooth move. Z's mouth went dry as she stretched her arms over her head, leaving the long line of her body bare for him. She ran her hands through her hair and tied it back into a tail, each movement seductive in its normalcy.

As normal as she could be, standing naked in the middle of a lit fucking pool area at nighttime where anyone could see her.

She dove into the pool, disappearing beneath the surface. Z stood there and stared as she cut through the water in sure strokes, working her way to the edge and turning to swim back the other way. He shook his head, the spell she'd created broken. He should stay where he was. She was as safe as she could possibly be on the property, so there was no reason for him to go down to the pool, except for wanting a closer look. That was inexcusable.

But it didn't stop him from tucking his phone into his pocket and making his way down the back staircase to the door leading into the pool. She was already on another go-round by the time he stepped into the humid space, appearing to take no notice of his presence. It shouldn't annoy him…but it did.

He sat on one of the lounge chairs near the steps out of the shallow end and waited. He couldn't take his eyes off her, the soothing sound of each stroke lulling him despite himself. Time seemed to stand still as she swam lap after lap, jarring back into motion when Sara stopped on the other side of the pool, watching him with eyes the same color as the water. "You take this protection detail awful seriously."

"You're Garrett's sister." He said that to remind himself as much as her.

"I am." She moved closer, the water shielding her body from him and yet offering tantalizing peeks at the same time. "But I was his sister in the back of that town car, and that didn't stop you."

"It was a mistake." He leaned forward, clasping his hands between his knees.

She reached a shallow enough depth to stand, stopping when the upper curve of her breasts showed. One small movement and he'd be able to see her nipples. He should look away. Should go back up to his room and lie on top of the bed and remember all the reasons why losing control risked ruining his life a second time.

But he didn't.

"What are you so afraid of? Garrett might be overprotective to the point of idiocy, but he knows better than to poke into my sex life."

"He's my friend."

"And?"

And Z had lost it all once before, hit rock bottom hard enough to drive away everyone and everything he cared about. He'd clawed his way out of the pit, one inch at a time, and carved out a life that he could be proud of. He'd be a fool of the worst sort to go through it all again, even for a woman like Sara. "I won't betray that."

"I'm not asking for you to put a ring on it and make an honest woman of me." As she spoke, she moved slowly toward him, coming out of the water like a modern day Aphrodite, revealing her breasts, her stomach, and finally the sweet spot between her thighs. "I just want you to relieve my boredom." She held up three fingers, as if he could focus on any point but where the water lapped at her pussy. "Just three little times."

"I thought you didn't want me to touch you."

"I was pissed." She shrugged. "I don't like rejection any more than the next person." She reached the steps and walked out of the water. "Please, Z. Play with me." She went to her knees. "Command me." And then to all fours. "Fuck me."

All the blood drained out of his head and rushed straight to his cock as she crawled toward him, her body one sinuous motion after another that seemed to somehow indicate the hottest of fucking, until she knelt between his thighs. He white-knuckled the chair arms as she started at his knees and stroked up this thighs, stopping just short of his cock. "Please."

If he said yes, it would take less than a heartbeat to take control. She'd welcome it—he could read that truth all over her face. He thought back to the car, to how sweetly she'd submitted, to how unbelievably hot it'd made him. If he agreed, he could have that again. He could take it all the way to its natural conclusion and take her any way he damn well pleased.

But she was Garrett's baby sister.

"No." Z lunged to his feet, knocking her onto her ass. Even though every instinct he had demanded he make sure she was okay, he forced himself to turn and stride away from her. If there was one woman on this earth off limits, it was Little Sara Reaver.

And she was the one woman he wanted more than his next breath.

Chapter Six

Sara spent a restless six hours in her bed before she gave sleep up for a lost cause. Her knees and butt were a little scraped from the concrete outside the pool, but it was her pride that stung the worst. She was well aware that her self-assurance bordered on arrogance, but she'd been half a second away from giving Z the blow job of his life and he'd knocked her on her ass in his rush to put as much distance between them as possible. It made her want to shred something.

Reject her once and she had no problem coming back swinging, even stoop to begging to get what she wanted. Reject her twice? No way. It was a done deal. She wasn't nearly masochistic enough to keep throwing herself at a man determined not to touch her.

No, he could just stay over in his side of this stupidly large house, and she'd stay here. Maybe they could work out some kind of kitchen schedule to really avoid each other.

As if thinking about food was all the reminder her

stomach needed, it growled. Loudly. Sara flopped back onto the bed. *Why him? Why couldn't they have picked some old, ugly grizzled friend of Uncle Rodger to keep me safe? Why did it have to be Z?*

As tempting as it was to hide in her room until her embarrassment faded, she wasn't willing to starve herself to avoid him. Which was a damn problem because she didn't have anything to wear. Sara had always seen clothing like a suit of armor—and armor was something she desperately needed right now.

She dug through the drawers of the dresser, but it was empty save for a short kimono-style robe that barely hit the tops of her thighs. Not something she should be wearing if she wanted to convince Z she was done trying to seduce him. But the only other option was to wear the dress she'd had on last night, and the memories now attached to *that* made her want to toss it into the nearest bonfire.

The robe it was.

She belted it as securely as possible and headed down to where she hoped the kitchen might be. Three wrong turns and more rooms than she wanted to count later, she finally found it. And it wasn't empty.

Z sat at the little nook table, annihilating a bowl of cereal. He didn't look up as she came into the room, just finished the bowl, got up, dumped it in the sink, and disappeared out the other door. Without so much as a fucking word or anything that would acknowledge her presence. Sara stared after him for entirely too long. Had she come down with the plague in the last six hours? Turned into a ghost? Because the only other explanation was that he was so pissed about what almost happened—twice—last night that he was ignoring her.

"Men." Needing to distract herself, she rummaged through the cabinets, finding enough food to feed a small army for a month. She grabbed a bunch of ingredients and arranged them on the counter. Cooking sounded really excellent just then, the more complicated the better. She'd make a delicious breakfast, and then maybe she'd bake cookies and something a little heartier, so she wouldn't have to leave her room for the rest of the day.

She couldn't—wouldn't—hide forever, but there was only so much of the silent treatment she could stand from a grown-ass man who should know better. Even thinking about it now made her blood pressure rise dangerously. She broke three eggs into a bowl and then grabbed a fork, whisking them hard enough to put them in danger of sloshing over the edge of the bowl. Then she set about chopping the onion and mushroom, muttering to herself as she did.

He was an idiot. That was the only explanation for him turning her down not once, but *twice*. He was attracted to her. He wouldn't have pulled that devastating Dom thing if he wasn't interested, and his body had more than spoken for itself. Last night in the pool, he'd been half a second from touching her. If he had, they'd be lounging naked in bed right now, instead of her in the kitchen by herself, cooking.

"Holy crap, what did he do?"

She looked up from behind the absurdly high pile of vegetables to find Ridley and Garrett standing in the doorway Z had left through earlier, shocked expressions on their faces. Her brother backed away slowly. "I'm going to…go get a report." And then the coward fled.

Ridley had no problem rounding the kitchen island to

hug her. "You're angry-cooking. Want to talk about it?"

She carefully set the knife on the chopping block. "If you want to whisk up the rest of the carton, yeah. I do." If she didn't talk to *someone*, she was bound to burst. God, she'd never felt so twisted up and off-center around anyone before, let alone a man. So she filled Ridley in while she cooked the sausage and sautéed the onions and mushrooms. "And then he just walked out of here this morning like I wasn't here."

Ridley turned sympathetic dark eyes on her. "He's being man-stupid."

"Well, I'm done with it. I know how to take a hint." She'd already practically begged him to fuck her. She wasn't going to give him the satisfaction of doing it again.

"You know, Garrett sometimes tells me stories about Z."

"I don't want to hear this."

"Yes, you do." Ridley stirred the food. "The man is almost godlike to his team. He won't ask them to do anything he won't do, and if it's at all possible, he takes the rougher missions so that they don't have to bear the burden of it. You know how Will and Garrett are control freaks?" She waited for Sara to shrug in agreement. "Well, Z blows them out of the water. If you'd told me you were going to set out to seduce him, I would have laughed in your face—lovingly, of course."

She snorted. "Of course."

"He's a tightly wound spring, and it sounds like you got through to him, whether he wanted it or not."

Sara rolled her eyes. "I didn't tie the man down and steal his virtue."

"No, but he lost control with you, however briefly. That's

got to scare the shit out of him."

Maybe. Or maybe it was all just an excuse to keep as much distance between them as possible. "I don't know. My pride is a delicate creature. It can only take so much abuse."

"Oh, please. You have pride enough to spare." Ridley grinned. "Besides, when has the great Sara Reaver ever met a wall she didn't go over, around, or through? Just think of Z as one giant, stubborn wall, and you're golden."

She speared a piece of the scramble with a fork and popped it in her mouth. Perfection. "A wall, huh?"

"Yep."

Her best friend sure knew what to say to light a fire under her ass. It had always been that way, even as far back as junior high. Sara had been just as unstoppable in her teens as she liked to think she was now. So why was she letting Z's issues stop her? He wanted her. He'd said as much before he suddenly decided to let her brother stand between them. She just needed to get his desire to override his potential guilt.

And she had just the plan.

Sara grabbed plates and dished up a portion. "Eat. Please tell me you brought clothes, because I need all the weapons I can fit in my arsenal."

Ridley snickered. "That's what she said."

...

The last person Z wanted to see after last night was Garrett, but he couldn't avoid the man. So he sat across from a coffee table in one of the house's countless rooms, and listened to his report. Truth be told, it was better than Z'd expected.

"Sounds like they want to scare her into submission."

"That's my thought. If they wanted to hurt her—" The big blond looked sick at the thought. "—they would have waited for her there. Even if she didn't go into the apartment, it would have been child's play to pick her up and toss her in a trunk. Or worse."

A single shot and all their problems would be permanently removed.

It made his stomach twist to even think about something hurting Sara. "Then her laying low will make them think they succeeded, and they should move on."

"Hopefully." Garrett sat back. "You okay? You look off."

Because he hadn't slept in well over twenty-four hours. Every time he closed his eyes, he saw Sara naked and crawling toward him, begging him to— Z cut off that thought before it could take root. Even with his friend right in front of him, he was hanging on by a thread. No one had roused him like Sara did—not even his ex-wife, who'd ultimately cost him everything. "I'm fine." He kept talking before Garrett could question him further. "I have Joe patrolling up the road, and Logan is taking the backwoods covering the rest of the property."

"Good. No one will get past those two." He hesitated. "If you need more manpower…"

The thought of being under the same house as Sara *and* Garrett for any length of time was unbearable. "Better that you stay in NYC and deal with the threat."

"Yeah, okay." But he was still watching Z too closely. "You keep her safe."

"I will." No outside threat would touch her. But who the hell was going to keep her safe from *him?*

They went over the next step a few times before he was satisfied. Garrett would take care of the work in NYC, combining his resources with Rodger Reaver. If those two couldn't make the city safe for Sara again, no one could. Z would stay here with her until the coast was clear—for however long it took. It was both heaven and hell knowing that he would be spending an unknown time in close quarters with her. He didn't like his chances of keeping himself in check for any amount of time, but he'd have to do it.

There was no other option.

They moved down to the kitchen, finding it empty except for a stack of Tupperware bowls with what looked like some sort of scramble in it. Garrett chuckled. "The only good thing about Sara being stressed is that she cooks. Just watch out for her temper—it's as vicious as her food is good."

Z had just a taste of it, and he could already confirm that. His jaw still ached a little bit from where she'd clocked him. "I'll keep that in mind."

"There you are!" Garrett's fiancée, Ridley, soared into the room and pressed a kiss to his lips as if they'd been separated for days instead of a single hour. Z ignored the surge of jealousy in his gut. He'd had that kind of intimacy and he'd lost it. He had no interest in trying for it again. At least, that's what he told himself whenever the longing got too overwhelming.

"How's Sara?" The question was out before he could think better of it.

"She's fine." Ridley gave him a look that raised the small hairs on the back of his neck and turned back to her fiancé. "I got everything unpacked for her. We should be heading back."

"I was planning on talking to my sister, baby."

"Since you have a penis, she's not currently interested." Ridley sailed out of the room, leaving Garret glaring after her.

He muttered under his breath, "She's going to pay for that one."

As glad as he was that his friend had found happiness, it physically *hurt* to see him with Ridley sometimes. When he was still smarting from his encounters with Sara? Yeah, that shit stung all the more. But he kept his feelings off his face with the ease of long practice. "Text when you get back to the city."

"Will do. I'll keep you updated all around."

"Good." It wasn't until he was alone in the kitchen again that he leaned against the counter and closed his eyes. *Fuck*. He had to fix things with Sara, one way or another. It had been difficult as hell to pretend to ignore her this morning, and he felt like shit while doing it. There had to be a way they could talk about this like adults. He'd explain to her all the reasons she was totally and completely off limits. She'd have to respect that.

No reason not to do it immediately. The faster they resolved this awkwardness between them, the better.

He made his way up the stairs to the room she'd chosen for her own. It sure as hell wasn't because he wanted to set eyes on her again. He knocked, waited, and got only silence as a response. Z knocked again. "Sara, I know you're in there."

Nothing.

Knowing he was breaking yet another rule, he tried the doorknob. It turned easily in his hand and he cracked the door to peek inside. She lay on the bed, surrounded by more pillows than one woman could possibly need, sound asleep. He opened the door a bit wider, taking in the fall of her blond hair, and the way she had wrapped her body around one of the larger pillows. It was all too easy to imagine her doing the same to *his* body.

With a silent curse, he backed out of the room, closing the door softly behind him. He'd let her sleep—their conversation could wait until she woke. Because, goddamn it, they *would* be having this conversation before another day went by.

Chapter Seven

Sara woke feeling refreshed and with new purpose. Tonight she'd successfully push Z over the edge, if it was the last thing she did. She'd figured out a plan as she was falling asleep earlier. Direct confrontation gave him the push he needed to walk away, so all she had to do was make him come to her. And then hopefully she'd just make him come.

She grinned and climbed off the bed. One of the things in the bag Ridley brought was a swimsuit, and she needed laps to take the edge off. Otherwise, she couldn't guarantee that she'd keep control of herself as long as necessary to get Z exactly where she wanted him. And it was increasingly vital that she get him where she wanted him.

He wasn't around as she dove into the water, but she swore she could feel his gaze on her from somewhere. Good. Hopefully he was remembering last night and sweating a little. It would serve him right.

Cutting through the water was a little slice of heaven

for her. It didn't calm her chaotic thoughts as much as usual, but it centered her. By the time she climbed out of the pool, she was ready. She went back up to her room and showered in the ridiculously large bathroom, taking the time to dry her hair and lotion up afterward until her skin positively gleamed. She opened the curtains to find that the sun had fully set, bathing the house in darkness.

Showtime.

She put on the robe and flipped on the lights in her room, the glare making it seem as if she had all the privacy in the world—when, in reality, anyone on the other side of the house could look through the window and see every detail.

She went to the tall oval mirror across from the bed and turned this way and that, checking her appearance. Perfect. Next was music. She set her iPod on the dock—another thoughtful gift from Ridley—and turned on her favorite, ZZ Ward. God, this music never failed to put her in the mood for a sweaty sex session.

Letting her eyes close, she raised her hands over her head and gave herself over to the music, careful to stay in the direct line of sight of the window. Her hips rolled with each beat, the robe coming slowly undone and finally slipping off her shoulders to the ground, leaving her naked.

It might be her imagination, but she was sure she could *feel* Z watching her, feel his eyes follow her hands as they cupped her breasts, playing with her nipples until they were hard points, and then sliding down her hips to her thighs. She parted her knees as she shimmied down to the ground, giving him the view of a lifetime, and then rolled her body up.

The song ended, quickly replaced by an even slower one, the throbbing beat seeming to take up residence between her legs. She crawled onto the bed and parted her legs wide, slipping her hand down to touch herself.

The phone rang.

Sara smiled as she circled her clit with one finger and reached for the phone with the other hand. She let it ring three times before answering, "I'm a bit busy."

Z actually growled. "Stop."

"No." It felt unnatural to deny him, but she wasn't afraid to play hardball right now. She'd bet that the only thing to get him over here was to blatantly disobey one of the orders he'd given her in the car on the way to the house, so that was exactly what she was going to do.

"Stop touching yourself *right fucking now*."

She dipped a finger inside and moaned a little. "If you don't like it, don't watch."

He took a harsh breath, as if he was actually going to yell at her, and she tensed. But his voice dropped. "You're trying to manipulate me."

"No, Sir." She used the term knowing it would drive him nuts. "I'm trying to get off—and you're distracting me."

"Don't you dare—"

She hung up, and tossed the phone off the bed, ignoring it when it immediately started ringing again. Let him twist while he watched her—she could already feel the pressure inside her ready to spike. She dug her heels into the mattress, stroking herself faster, and used her free hand to pinch her nipple like Z had in the car. Thinking about him, about how she'd felt when his harsh words commanded her, was enough to have her teetering on the edge. She moaned.

Her door flew open hard enough to bounce off the wall. She froze, opening her eyes to find Z towering at the end of her bed, his expression thunderous. He looked like some sort of demon who was going to either give her the greatest pleasure of her life or punish her for every offense.

She sure as hell hoped he'd do both.

"You." He grabbed her ankle and dragged her to the edge of the mattress. She had a wild moment of panic and struggled, kicking him in the shoulder with her free foot, but he growled and caught her other ankle, spreading her legs wide enough to hurt. "I gave you clear instructions."

Any response she might have come up with—and there were a few choice ones—died in her throat. This was what she'd wanted, but she'd made a horrible mistake by pushing him past the point of no return. "Z—"

"Silence." His tone brooked no argument. "You thought I was making empty threats, sweetheart?" He dragged her further off the bed, until her ass was only halfway on the mattress. "You should know better. Tell me your safe word."

"Wolfman." The word was barely more than a whisper.

He flipped her in one smooth move, pinning her to the bed with a hand on the back of her neck. "Did you come?"

She pushed against his hold, but she wasn't going anywhere unless he took her there. She'd thought she felt heat from her impending orgasm, but it was a tiny campfire compared to the inferno blazing through her now. "No, Sir."

"I would be disappointed in you if you did." His hand came down on her ass, hard enough for her breath to catch in her throat. "But you intended to come, even if you didn't reach it." Another slap on the other cheek. "I promised that any disobedience would be punished, and it will be."

She bit her lip hard enough she was worried she'd taste blood, fighting against the urge to beg him to punish her, to fuck her, to do whatever he damn well pleased with her. He shoved two fingers into her, making her cry out. Z cursed. "So wet. You're close."

It wasn't a question, so she didn't respond, but apparently he didn't need her words for confirmation. He withdrew his fingers and delivered another devastating slap to her ass, and then another, as if he couldn't stand the thought of the cheeks receiving uneven treatment. "Sweetheart, the only time you're coming tonight is when you're coming around my cock."

...

Everything had ceased to exist for Z the second Sara's robe hit the floor. He'd watched with growing agitation as she'd touched herself, as she climbed on the bed with the obvious intent of masturbating, and everything peaked when she'd directly disobeyed him. It didn't matter that he had no right to this woman or that just today he'd promised himself to put this all behind him.

He couldn't let that kind of bullshit stand.

And now here she was, bent over the bed, her ass red from his hand, her pussy so wet it had been a fight to stop finger-fucking her. He was out of control with no hope of stopping, and he damn well knew it. "I'm going to fuck you, do you understand?"

"Yes, Sir." Her voice was partially muffled by the mattress, but he heard her clearly enough.

Z palmed her between her legs. "If you want to stop, use your fucking safe word now. Because I'm going to be inside you within ten seconds."

She flailed, and he loosened his grip on the back of her neck until she could twist around and meet his gaze. "Make it five seconds, Sir."

Fuck.

He undid his pants with one hand, pausing to grab the condom out of his pocket before he kicked them off. "You're a mouthy little sub, aren't you? Do you know what mouthy little subs get?"

"A mouthful of cock?" She hissed out a breath when he spanked her again. "Sir."

"You will—when I decide to allow it. Be good and I'll let you suck me off." He tore open the condom and rolled it on one-handed, never taking his gaze from her opening. Shit, she was so damn little. If he wasn't careful, he'd break her. "Hands on the mattress. Push yourself up." He guided her forward until she was on all fours on the bed. It put her pussy exactly where he wanted it. He leaned down and drew his tongue up her center, delighting in her cry as much as he did in her taste. She was soft and wet and welcoming and everything he could have dreamed of.

He sucked on her clit and moved on before she could do more than whimper, thrusting his tongue inside her. She was ready for him, probably had been the moment he charged into her room. He stood and yanked her back so that her feet hit the floor. She barely had time to brace herself when he thrust into her in one smooth stroke.

Z reclaimed his hold on the back of her neck and thrust into her again, cursing at how good it felt. Words rose as he fucked her, "You wanted this. You've wanted this since last night in the car. You would have fucked me right then, let me thrust into your tight little pussy, and then begged for more." Her hands clawed the comforter, her breath sobbing from her throat, and still he didn't stop his relentless assault.

"And the pool. Fuck, woman, you would have sucked my cock right then without shame."

"Yes, Sir." She moved as much as he'd allow, taking him even deeper.

"I like that you have no shame, sweetheart. In fact, I fucking love it." She cried out, her pussy tightening around his cock as she came, her body tensing as wave after wave hit. He pulled out before she could pull him over the edge with her and thrust two fingers into her, needing to feel her lose control, needing to feel her tighten around him again. It wasn't enough. Fuck, it wasn't even close to enough.

Totally and completely out of control, Z flipped her again, shoving her onto the bed and falling onto her pussy like a starving man. He spoke against her heated flesh in between licks. "I didn't give you permission to come." He flicked her clit over and over again until her back arched. "Do it again."

Her hands were on the back of his head holding him to her, but he wouldn't stand for even that much. Z pinned her wrists on either side of her hips and kept going, driving her wild until she let loose a scream, coming against his face. He kept working her until she was limp and panting, totally spent. He crawled up to lean against the headboard and pulled her into his arms, letting her ragged breathing soothe him as little else could. This session had barely taken the edge off, but he needed her to realize who was in control.

Because there was no going back now.

She finally sighed, and he could feel her smile against his chest. "Not bad for number one."

"Sara." He looped his hand through her hair and used it to bring her face up to his. "I didn't come." He kept going even as her eyes went wide. "I'm nowhere near done with you."

Chapter Eight

Z wasn't even close to done with her.

It should delight Sara to know that—it was what she wanted, after all—but there was a curious numbness building in her chest. She was in trouble. Deep, deep trouble. And she wanted to go deeper. So she nodded against his hold. His grin was a reward in and of itself. "Good girl."

It's only three times, she reminded herself. It didn't matter if she lapped up his praise like it was better than chocolate, because this had a clear and concrete expiration date. There had to be.

He set her on the bed and stood. "Lie on your back with your hands laced behind your neck." He waited for her to obey. "Do not move." Then he walked out of the room.

She craned her neck, but there was nothing to see. It felt unnatural to lie there when her body was already recovering from those mind-blowing orgasms. She itched to get up, to move, to do *something*. But he'd said not to move, and she was more curious to see what he had planned than what her punishment would be if she got up. She shifted, her ass still smarting from the spanking he'd delivered.

A few minutes later, he returned, two belts in his hand. She went still, her heart skipping at the sight. Was he going to beat her again? She wasn't afraid of pain, but it didn't do much for her if there wasn't pleasure attached. Sara opened her mouth to tell him just that, but at the last second remembered his command to be silent and didn't say anything.

He surveyed her, as if checking to see if she was in the exact same position he'd left her. Apparently satisfied, he climbed onto the bed and straddled her ribs. He took her left hand and looped the belt around her wrist. "This won't hold you unless you want it to." He met her gaze. "*I* want it to. If your hands leave their bindings, you will be punished."

The man sure as hell had a lot of rules. Her breath hitched as he fastened the belt to the bedpost, and then repeated the process with her right hand. She gave them an experimental tug. His knots would hold enough for her to yank on them with all her strength, but the loops were wide enough to slip her hand in and out of without difficulty. She gripped the leather and waited.

Z sat back, his weight on his heels rather than her, his cock an impressive length just out of reach of her mouth. "You have exquisite breasts." He pinched her nipples hard enough to have her back arching off the mattress. "You won't cover them up for the remainder of our contract."

Sara shook her head, trying to focus. What did he… The truth hit her in the stomach. He wanted her naked and ready for him whenever he chose to take her. She shivered at the thought. If anyone came out here, they'd see her walking around naked, see Z doing whatever he wanted to her. She clenched her thighs together.

"Now, sweetheart, do you think you've been good enough to suck my cock?"

Probably not, but that wasn't going to stop her. She nodded vigorously. "Yes, Sir."

He laughed. "Eager, aren't you?" He leaned forward, putting one hand on the headboard and using the other to guide his cock between her lips. She didn't waste any time lifting her head and sucking him as deep as she could in this position. Working him with her tongue and lips, she moaned. God, she needed more, so much more.

Z pumped into her mouth, transferring one hand to the back of her head, controlling even this. His low curse was music to her ears and she tightened her grip on the belts, because it was all too tempting to touch him, to run her hands up this big thighs, to cup his balls, to supplement her oral strokes with manual ones.

"Enough." He backed up, ignoring the sound of protest she made. He grabbed a second condom and rolled it on while she watched. Every move the man made was precise, exerting just enough effort to get what he wanted done. So carefully controlled, even when he was in the midst of a haze of lust. She wanted him between her thighs again, buried deep inside her as he drove them both to finish.

He must have been thinking the same thing, because he braced himself on his elbows and pushed into her, one slow inch at a time. "This is one, Sara. Don't think for a second that you're going to get off so easy with the other two." He sheathed himself to the hilt, holding perfectly still. "Wrap your legs around me."

She was only too happy to obey. He took her mouth, kissing her like both their lives depended on it as he rolled his hips, grinding against her clit while he was impossibly deep inside her. She gripped the belts so tightly, she was sure she'd have imprints on her palms, but she refused to let go, even though she wanted to touch him almost more than she wanted her next orgasm.

"Now." Z buried his hands in her hair, sucking on her neck. "Come for me now."

As if her body had been awaiting his command, it exploded, a breathless scream tearing itself from her mouth as she came. She kept her legs tightly around him as he cursed and thrust hard into her, following her over the precipice. Her body shook so hard, it was all she could do to lie there and ride it out.

He gentled his kisses against her neck and nipped her earlobe. "You pleased me tonight."

The warmth in her chest had no place, even in this situation. It was only sex. Outstanding, forget-your-own-name sex, but sex all the same. Even with the power games, she had no business wanting to curl up around him and sleep. That was crossing so many lines, Sara didn't even know where to start.

She had to put up some boundaries. Now.

・・・

Z could actually feel her trying to withdraw from him while he was still buried inside her. He'd made the mistake of tolerating that shit with his ex—he wasn't about to do it with Sara. He lifted his head and forced her to meet his gaze. Sure enough, those blue eyes were already shaking off the pleasure and looking wary.

He had a choice now. He could push her, either until she gave in or until something broke, or he could back off and give them both some breathing room.

Since Z wasn't feeling the least bit settled right then, he chose the latter. He climbed off her, and pulled her to her feet after him. She opened her mouth, but he shook his head. If either of them started talking right then, they were bound to say something they'd regret.

He wasn't sure that would be a bad thing, though.

Before he could think too closely on that, he towed her into the oversized bathroom and turned on the shower. He tested the water, and turned to find her watching him with a strange look on her face. "What?"

"I don't know. This is just…"

Strange. Unexpected. Completely fucked.

He kept the words internal. It wasn't her job to shoulder his baggage, but hell if he'd expected *this*. She'd taken everything he'd given her and come back begging for more. He searched her face, looking for signs of regret or, worse, fear—the two major things he'd missed in Jennifer—but there was nothing except a strange mix of contentment and worry that was mirrored in the emotions twining through him in that moment. "Yeah."

"Maybe it would be better if we did this separately."

She was probably right, but he wasn't ready to let her walk out yet, so Z held open the shower door and motioned her to precede him. With a sigh, she obeyed the silent command.

The shower was big enough for four people, and the dual showerheads gave them plenty of room to maneuver.

As much as he wanted to keep touching her, he stayed on his side, scrubbing himself down and watching her do the same.

"You're staring." She turned and tipped her face up to the spray, letting the soap wash off her body in paths his hands itched to follow.

He didn't bother to deny it. Instead, he let the hot water beat into his skin in a vain effort to release the tension there. Opposing urges rose inside him, the need to haul her ass to his room to sleep in his bed, to touch her and fuck her and make her his in the only way he could.

And to walk out of this bathroom and do something—anything—to get his head back on straight.

Neither option was the right one. He'd tried avoiding her, and that had worked for a less than twenty-four hours. Z called things like they were, and he didn't like his chances of keeping his hands off her for the remainder of their time here. It was a losing battle, and a waste of effort. He wanted her. She wanted him. There was no point in spending precious energy fighting the inevitable.

Hell, he didn't *want* to fight it.

So he chose neither and settled for a middle of the road option. "Have dinner with me."

Sara raised her eyebrows. "Dinner."

"Yeah."

"Did you forget that we're on house arrest in the middle of nowhere?"

"No." He shut off his water, and reached around to shut off hers as well. "But I happen to know someone cooked a whole hell of a lot of food earlier. I can work a microwave as well as the next man." He leaned forward, tracking the drop of water trailing down her collarbone and over her breast.

"I'll even get out a candle and make it truly fancy."

"Be still my heart." A tentative smile pulled at the edges of her lips. "I guess I did work up something of an appetite."

"Thought so." He grabbed two towels and handed her one. As tempting as it was to dry her off himself, to spend all the time he wanted exploring every inch of her body, it wouldn't do a damn thing for his control. So he kept his distance, drying off efficiently and walking back into the bedroom to pull on his pants. He turned in time to see her shrug into the tiny robe she'd been wearing earlier, the bottom of it barely hitting the tops of her thighs. It was all too easy to imagine going to his knees in front of her, drawing back the silky fabric and...

Z looked away. *Keep it together, Loreto.*

He followed her out of the bedroom and down the stairs, struggling to keep his thoughts away from all the available surfaces to press Sara against and fuck her until he forgot all the reasons this was a terrible idea. To distract himself, he started talking, "How long have you worked for your uncle?"

"I would think that'd be in the file you're sure to have on me."

"I don't have a file on you." When she shot him a look over her shoulder, he amended, "I don't have an exhaustive file on you." There hadn't been much time to get this place put together, let alone to gather all the information he usually would on a body he or his men were guarding. Add in the fact that this was Garrett's sister, and he'd been reluctant to dig too deeply on her. The man was entitled to his secrets and, as his family, so was she.

"And what does this non-exhaustive file say?" She walked into the kitchen and went straight to the fridge to pull out several stacks of Tupperware.

"Do you want some help?"

She waved him away. "Sit. This will only take a minute. And stop trying to change the subject."

Z leaned forward, propping his elbows on the counter. "If you were charged with guarding someone, or setting it up, what information would you put in there?"

She paused. "Is this some weird way of answering without answering?"

"I'm curious." He'd only met Rodger Reaver a few times, but he was a man who would fit on Z's team. He was competent and smart and had a ruthless streak that Z could admire. He might have given Garrett training, but the Army had done a lot of that, too. But Rodger had Sara working under him for years. To hear tell of it, he was grooming her to take over the company when he finally retired.

She'd been off her game for the last two days, but she hadn't let being caught off-guard slow her down after that first time. It was impressive, really. And he found himself wanting to know more, to see more.

"Okay, fine, I'll play. I'd get every bit of information that linked up my client with the person or entity that wanted to see them dead. Knowing the *why* behind it could be useful, especially since it could potentially tell me how far the enemy is willing to go in order to take them out—and how hard my people are going to have to work to keep the client alive." She dumped several of the bowls into a large saucepan, turned on the heat, and then covered it.

"Then I'd look into what would make my client problematic. Do they have any addictions, any history of stupid behavior, any red flags that would mean my job making sure the idiot didn't end up dead would be harder than normal." She tapped her finger against her lip. "I might look into what their weaknesses and interests were, too. You want to make the situation as comfortable as you can, while still being safe, so they don't get twitchy and decide to take a jaunt somewhere that would complicate the situation."

He found he liked listening to her reason it out. He'd known she was smart, but seeing it was something else altogether. Z sat back to keep from reaching for her. "That about sums it up."

"Really? And here I thought you'd have the name of the guy I lost my virginity to or what my favorite food is. I'm very disappointed."

"I can see that." He shook his head, smiling despite himself. "Why don't you fill in the blanks then, since my file is so lacking?"

"Yeah, no, I don't think I'll make it that easy on you." Her eyes lit up. "You first."

He didn't pretend to misunderstand. "I'm not a sharer."

"Funny, neither am I. It's tit for tat, Z." With a grin that kicked him right in the chest, she turned back to check the pan and stir it.

Would it really hurt to share such harmless information? Just because they talked didn't mean they'd traipse through ancient history that was better left untouched. He watched her set a kettle on the stove. "Okay, I'll play." He thought back over the two questions she'd brought up. Easy enough to answer. "I lost my virginity to a sweet girl named Hilary. My favorite food is Mexican."

"Was it any good?"

"Mexican is always good."

She laughed, the sound high and bright and perfectly Sara. "That's not what I meant and you know it."

Yeah, he did. But he liked hearing her laugh. It made him want to do or say something to draw out that sound again. Instead, he answered her question. "I thought it was, though I've learned a thing or two since then."

Her grin widened. "I imagine so."

"Your turn, sweetheart."

"His name was Stephen and he wasn't a sweet boy, and my favorite food is paella." She hopped onto the counter next to the stove. "Okay, this could be fun. Why did you start the whole mercenary business? You seem like you would have fit in just fine with the normal military."

He had. He had fucking loved it. But the choice had been taken away because of one shitty decision. It wasn't something he was going to get into now, though. "Men like me—like your brother—sometimes have a hard time fitting back into society after the service. I floundered a bit, but when I looked around, I realized there was a need that I was uniquely qualified to meet."

"And that's...it? You were qualified and so you stepped up?"

It sounded foolish when she said it like that. Z crossed his arms over his chest, giving the idea more thought than he had in years. "I like what I do. More than that, if I wasn't the one doing it, someone else would be—and they'd be doing a shittier job of it. I make sure we only take missions that don't compromise my men." Though he wasn't above taking those missions himself on occasion. "And I stack the deck as best I can to make sure they get home safely." The explanation still felt inadequate, but Sara nodded like she understood, so he asked, "And you? Why the fixer business?"

"Because there are far too many problems in this world that don't have easy fixes. Or any fixes at all." She eyed the saucepan. "I think Uncle Rodger had a similar experience to yours when he got out of the service. He might be a right bastard on occasion, but he's got an honorable streak a mile wide. Growing up with him was like knowing a real life hero." She shrugged. "I guess some of that rubbed off on me. I like puzzles. I like taking a seemingly impossible situation and twisting it to my client's benefit. I like the relief and gratitude in their eyes when I can deliver on my promises."

"Seems you have a little bit of a heroic streak, yourself."

"Nah. I'll leave that to folk like you and my brother and my uncle." Sara crossed her legs, drawing his attention to the long line of skin disappearing under the bottom of her robe.

He wanted her. Fuck, he wanted her more than he'd wanted something in a very long time. But, strangely enough, he wanted to continue this conversation more than he wanted to bury himself between her legs. "What else do you want to know?" A bold question—reckless even.

A strange look passed over her face, something like fear. "I think that's enough for now. The food's ready."

Chapter Nine

Sara couldn't believe she'd let herself get drawn into such a potentially exposing conversation with Z. Sure, they hadn't talked about anything particularly revealing, but she still felt a little raw. A little vulnerable. Because, for just a few minutes, she'd forgotten that this man was one she was sleeping with. There was a place for friends who she spilled out her heart to, and a place for men who drove her out of her mind with pleasure like Z had done earlier.

And ne'er the two shall meet.

Except she…liked talking to him. Even as she dumped half the stir-fry into a bowl and slid it across the island to him, she wanted to ask him more questions, to find out more about him. Doing so meant revealing more of herself, though, and she couldn't do that. He already knew too much.

Sex was so much easier. There was no need for heart to hearts or finding out that he liked Mexican food and had a hero complex to rival her brother's. There was no excuse for her curiosity. None.

She took a bite to distract herself, but all it did was give her more opportunity to study him. He watched her just as closely, an unreadable look on his face. She found she liked those pale green eyes of his, liked how they were such a contrast to the rest of him and yet managed to fit him perfectly.

She wanted to know what got him kicked out of the military. Sara couldn't imagine what it could have been. From the tone of his voice and the look on his face when he skated over that particular conversational landmine, his discharge hadn't been by choice. He didn't move like someone injured, so she doubted it was honorable discharge related to some kind of wartime injury.

So what was it?

She stamped down her curiosity and focused on eating. It was none of her business. Yes, they were sleeping together—at least for now—but that didn't mean he owed her a truth that was obviously a painful one. She sure as hell wasn't going to tell him about her hopes and fears.

But a part of her wanted to.

She'd been going it alone for so long, she couldn't remember the last time she'd had a conversation like this, let alone with someone who wasn't family or Ridley. The uncomfortable thought rose that maybe she'd *never* gone there before.

Calm down, idiot. It's not like you gave him the key to your soul. It was just a silly little talk about things that you don't talk to anyone about. No big deal.

She finished her bowl and moved to the sink to wash it out. It gave her the illusion of space, but she could feel Z's gaze on the back of her neck. If she were smart, she'd do something to turn this back to sex and the comfortable box she'd created. Instead, all she wanted to do was flee.

"So—" She turned around and let loose an embarrassingly girly scream when she found him six inches away. "What the hell? Give me the courtesy of making some damn noise when you move."

He reached around her to set his bowl in the sink, bringing them nearly chest-to-chest. "We need to talk about hard limits."

This, she could do. This was just sex. Sara ignored how much that term felt like a lie and leaned against the counter. "Easy—nothing beyond light pain play, no age play, no furries." She hesitated, then plunged on. "I'm also not into sharing."

"If at any point, you want to update the list, tell me immediately."

"I will. You know, I *have* done this kind of thing before."

A small smile pulled at the edges of his lips. "I'm aware. Now, one more question, sweetheart."

She didn't *want* any more questions. It was startlingly easy to talk to him, and God only knew what would come out of her mouth if she let her guard down. She kind of *liked* Z. She liked how quiet he was, and how closely he seemed to watch everything around him.

Oh yeah, and she liked how he could command her body as if she belonged to him and him alone.

It was that last thing that had her sliding sideways, needing more space between them. "I'm tired of this game."

"What are you so afraid of?"

She opened her mouth to say she wasn't afraid of a single damn thing, but it was a lie. There were plenty of things she was afraid of, things that she wasn't about to utter aloud. So she deflected, "This has been fun, but you wore me out and I'm going to bed."

She made it a full step before his voice stopped her in her tracks. "My room." *Absolutely not.* She spun, but he was already speaking again, "That wasn't a request."

"The only place you get to order me around is in the bedroom." She might play the role of sub when it suited her, but she wasn't looking for the deeper role that some people craved. She didn't need a Dom in every aspect of her life, interfering and generally being a pain in the ass.

"You gave yourself to me until our timeline runs out. Unless you've changed your mind."

The arrogant ass knew she'd done no such thing. This whole situation might tread right on the line of making her want to run for the hills, but she wanted the way he made her feel more than she wanted to protect herself from potential hurt. She glared. "I'm not a coward."

"I never said you were."

Maybe not, but she was starting to feel like one for being worried. *It'll be okay. I have this under control.*

Right.

...

As soon as she nodded, Z was moving. He didn't want to give her a chance to change her mind. Without saying a word, he scooped her up and headed for his bedroom. He chose not to comment on her muttering dark things under her breath. She'd agreed to his demand, had chosen to continue this instead of calling the whole thing off. She was entitled to some muttering if it made her feel better.

Plus, he liked the feeling of her in his arms. She was soft and welcoming and her hair draped over his shoulder when she finally gave up and rested her head there. He reached his room all too soon, and nudged open the door with his foot. It looked much the same as every other room in this place, but he found the cool gray walls and black furniture soothing.

He shifted his grip on her, pulled down the bedding, and set her down. "You'll sleep with me until this ends."

"*Sleep?*" She crossed her arms over her breasts. "You're already done for the night? Pity. I guess you aren't as young as you used to be."

He stared until she dropped her gaze. "That was your one pass, sweetheart."

"Stop calling me that."

"No." He sat on the opposite corner of the bed, keeping the distance between them. She'd wanted this, but now she was uncomfortable, and he wanted to know why. "This bothers you."

She drew her knees up to her chest, still looking down. "A lot of things bother me."

"But this bothers you more than most. Why?"

"I thought we were done playing twenty questions. My Sir commands it, and so I obey."

He recognized the ploy for what it was, but that didn't mean her words left him unaffected. "As you should. But right now your Sir is commanding answers."

"Why?"

The question had merit. No matter how possessive he currently felt about her, this couldn't last. She'd put a limit on them, and he'd agreed to it. They might fit together unbelievably well in the bedroom, he might like talking with her a whole hell of a lot more than he should, but they led different lives. He was down in Baltimore, and she was in New York. But, more than that, she had her entire life ahead of her. He was on his second chance. A woman like her deserved better than he could offer.

But he still wanted to know. "Because I want them. Now, tell me."

She sighed, her internal conflict written all over her face. Clearly she wanted to tell him to fuck off. Hell, he might deserve it. There was nothing in their verbal contract that covered him traipsing all over her emotional hot buttons. If he were smart, he'd let her go back to her own room, and keep this thing restricted to sex and sex alone.

Knowing that didn't stop him from sitting there and waiting her out, though.

Finally, she relented. "I don't sleep over."

He expected her to keep talking, but that seemed all she intended to give up. "You never sleep over?"

"No." A shrug. "What's the point? Any guy I sleep with knows the rules — three times. There's no need to pretty it up or try to get intimate outside of having sweaty naked fun." Sara still wouldn't meet his gaze. She picked at a thread in the comforter. "I don't like it."

He leaned against the footboard, considering. Z had known this woman had walls — like called to like, after all — but it was only now becoming clear just how high they were. She'd been hurt in the past, because a person didn't simply come up with rules like hers without reason. He wanted to know who'd hurt her so horribly, even though he damn well knew he had no right to the knowledge. "Your rule of three isn't just for me."

"It's an overarching thing." She still wouldn't look at him, but her body was so tense, she seemed half a second from shattering and running from the room.

Z hadn't had a submissive under his command since the one that had ended so badly, but he sometimes had to stake his life and the lives of his men on his ability to read a person or situation. He'd pushed Sara as far as he could tonight without breaking something—and he might like rough bedroom games, but he didn't want to actually hurt her. "Okay."

"Okay?"

"Thank you for answering my question honestly—all my questions." He shucked off his pants and got beneath the covers on the opposite side of the bed. Since it was a king, even with his size, there was an ocean of space between them. He waited for her to do the same, and then shut off the light and lay down, the light of the pool casting strange patterns on the ceiling. "Come here." If she feared intimacy, he could give her the one thing she'd accept—lust.

It was playing dirty, and he damn well knew it, but the thought of being in the same bed as her and *not* having his arms around her was too much to bear. If the only thing she'd allow him was sex based, then he'd use that to his own ends.

She slid over to lie next to him, her body as stiff as a board. He wasted no time pulling her so her back rested against his chest, her wonderfully curved ass tucked against his already hard cock. She jerked. "I take back the old man comment."

He grinned, amused despite himself. "I appreciate that."

Before she could move away or say anything else, he slipped his hand down to hook around her knee and lift it up so her foot rested on the bed behind his legs, leaving her open for him. "I wasn't lying earlier when I said I was far from done with you."

He kissed the back of her neck, biting the sensitive tendon there, and cupped her pussy. "Wet again, sweetheart? You're damn near as insatiable as I am."

"Don't take it personally. It's been awhile." And she was obviously still pissed.

"You wound me." He took his time, exploring her with his fingers, parting her folds and delving inside, moving on to circle her clit, and then starting all over again. It wasn't enough to get her off and he damn well knew it, but he liked her little indrawn breaths when his palm slid over her clit and the way she shook when he pushed two fingers inside her.

Z shifted, sliding his other arm beneath her and rolled back enough that he could cup her breast, her body totally open to him. As he circled her nipple while keeping up his exploration between her legs, one of her arms reached back to touch him. He grabbed her wrist. "No."

"But—"

If he let her touch him, he wouldn't maintain the tightrope of control he currently walked. He couldn't afford to forget that he wasn't fucking her again tonight. "No." He slid his fingers inside her and used his other hand to roll her clit between his fingers.

She cried out. "Z, I'm going to—"

"Not yet." He moved up to cup both breasts, touching her nipples how he already knew she liked, keeping her on the edge, but not enough to push her over. Her hips squirmed, ass rubbing against his cock in a way that made him groan. "The things you do to me. You don't even know."

"I think I have some idea."

Enough. He couldn't hold on any longer and still maintain his goal to *not* drive his cock deep inside her again. He bit the back of her neck and shoved two fingers into her. "Ride me, sweetheart." He growled when she instantly moved to obey. "Yeah, just like that."

"Z."

"You have permission." He squeezed her nipple and she cried out, her pussy milking his fingers as she came apart around him. A part of him resented the darkness of the room and their position, keeping her expression hidden from him, but she needed this more than he did at this point. It was a gift, the only kind she was willing to take.

The only kind he was able to give her.

He gentled his touches and finally moved his hand up to cup her hip. The curve fit the palm of his hand as if made for him. Z tried to dismiss the thought, not so far gone that he didn't realize the danger of it. Sara wasn't his, not in any kind of permanent way. But he would take care of her while they were together. "Now, sleep."

She laughed hoarsely. "You can't just command me to sleep and have it happen."

He kissed her behind her ear, inhaling her lily scent and reminding himself for the millionth time that he couldn't take this any farther than he already had. He'd lived through worse than a devastating case of blue balls before, and he had no doubt that he would again. "Sleep."

A few minutes passed, and he listened to her breathing

in the darkness. It struck him that he hadn't shared a bed with another person since his ex. Apparently he and Sara had more in common than he'd guessed, though he'd bet their reasons weren't even close to the same.

He was almost asleep when he heard her whisper, "Thank you, Sir." Z slipped from wakefulness with a small smile on his face.

Chapter Ten

Sara woke up with her cheek pressed against a moving pillow. She cracked open an eye, taking in the miles of dark skin that was Z's chest. *I'm sleeping on Z's chest.* Oh God, this was so far from okay, it wasn't even funny. She had to move right now. But when she tried to scoot away, he stopped her with a hand on her elbow, trapping her in position.

"Morning."

"Uh, morning." What was she supposed to do or say? The only person she ever had actual sleepovers with was Ridley, and she never had to worry about waking up wrapped around the brunette like some sort of strangler monkey.

She needed time and space, and it didn't look like he was going to give her either. Sure enough, he ran a hand down her spine, drawing her close yet. "I have big plans for you today."

She closed her eyes in relief. Sex, she could do. And, if it knocked another of the three times off the list, that was for the best. She simultaneously loved and hated how Z made her feel—like she could spend years kneeling at his feet, obeying his will. It wasn't an option. She'd seen what happened when people got embroiled in relationships—nothing but trouble. If her parents' clusterfuck of a breakup had taught her anything, it was that you couldn't rely on other people not to change while you weren't looking. Sure, they might fit up great now, but there was no guaranteeing they would continue to do so as the years went on. Hell, even her twin brothers—two people she'd been *sure* would never go and shift on her had done exactly that. No, it was easier to keep things in clear, concise boundaries where they ended before anything got too heavy.

Which was a problem, because things were *already* too heavy with Z. It was worse, in a way, because she'd asked for it and, now that she'd gotten what she thought she wanted, she felt like she was drowning.

Or suffocating.

"But first, I have a question."

Not more questions. Sara pulled away, struggling when he kept a hold of her. "Stop, Z. I can't breathe." She fought harder, a panicked bird in a cage, with no hope of escape. "*Please.*"

"Look at me."

She couldn't. If she obeyed, she'd be lost. She'd forget all the reasons why she never should have asked for this. He'd pin her with those green eyes and she'd start spouting all the things that she worked so hard to keep inside. She'd tell him anything he wanted to know. So she closed her eyes and did the one thing guaranteed to grant her freedom. "Wolfman. Wolfman, Wolfman, *Wolfman.*"

Instantly, Z let go of her, allowing her to scramble off the bed. She took the sheet with her, which was yet another in a long string of mistakes, because it left him sprawled on the bed, naked and too tempting for her state of mind. She simultaneously wanted to crawl back and let him comfort her, and to run screaming from the room. She wrapped the sheet around her, needing some sort of shield, even one so flimsy as this.

He propped himself up on his elbows, green eyes concerned, but didn't make any other moves toward her. "What's wrong?"

"Nothing."

"Sara, you just panicked and safed out. Tell me why. Was it the question or the waking up in my bed?" When she still hesitated, he sighed. "How am I supposed to keep from repeating the mistake if I don't know what I did?"

That sounded suspiciously logical, when she was feeling anything but. She backed toward the door. "You don't have to worry about making the same mistake, because this is over. I thought I could do this, but I can't."

He narrowed his eyes, watching her retreat as if measuring how fast he could cross the distance between them. "You're scared. Terrified."

Hell yes, she was. Because there was still a part of her clamoring to climb back into bed with him and never leave. The only reason her love life didn't interfere with the *rest* of her life was because she kept it carefully boxed. After last night and this morning, it was painfully clear that no box would contain Z—or her conflicting feelings about him. One night of sleeping next to a man shouldn't be enough to spook her this much, but it did.

Because it opened up all sorts of things she worked really hard not to think about.

Like how good Z looked in the morning, with his eyes still hazy from sleep, his defenses down for the first time since they'd met. And how nice it had been to make up dinner last night while they talked, and how she'd discovered his unexpected sense of humor. Or what a lazy day with him would look like, breakfast and sex and submission and... No. She couldn't do it. So she said so. "I can't do this."

"You already said that." He sat up, and frowned when she startled. "I'm not going to attack you."

It was on the tip of her tongue to ask what he called last night, but she couldn't dirty that experience, even jokingly. "I need space." More space than was possible with them both stuck in this house, massive or not. She reached the doorway. "I'm sorry. I just... I have to go."

"*Stop*." Her feet froze, and she couldn't keep going, no matter how much her mind screamed not to obey him. His voice came from behind her. "Look at me."

She turned, stiff and unyielding, to find him less than a step away. God, he moved fast when he wanted to—fast and silent. Sara made a sound that might have been a whimper. "Please, Z."

He reached out and cupped the back of her neck, and all the fight went out of her as if he'd pushed a magic button. Her knees buckled, and she might have fallen if he hadn't caught her. For his part, he didn't look any happier with this change of events than she was, but he picked her up and carried her back to the bed. "We'll talk. If I'm satisfied by the end of it, you can get back to fleeing my presence."

...

Z hated how stiff Sara was in his arms, but he wasn't about to let her run without some sort of explanation. He had an idea he knew what the source of her issues were—he hadn't been Garrett's friend for so many years without picking up bits and pieces of the man's past—but he wanted to hear her say it. Because if he was wrong, and she was hurt or upset about what had happened between them last night, then he needed a chance to make it right.

His stomach lodged itself somewhere in his throat at the thought of causing her harm. She'd seemed right there in the moment with him, but so had Jennifer up until the moment she cried foul. He'd missed he signs with his ex. He wasn't going to make the same mistake with Sara.

She hadn't shown any regret or fear last night, but he'd learned the hard way that a new day could bring everything into a completely different light. If Sara hated him for what they'd done... Fuck, he could barely stand the thought.

He sank onto the overstuffed chair near the window and tucked her head against his shoulder. Sometimes things were easier to talk about when you weren't looking directly at a person. She didn't relax one bit, so he started, "Are you hurt?"

"What?" She jerked back to meet his gaze.

Each word felt like it was a shard of glass in his chest. "Did I hurt you?"

He found himself holding his breath as her confusion cleared and her eyes went wide. "No. Last night was amazing—better than amazing."

Some of the tension left him. This was about the intimacy of sleeping next to him, then. That, he could deal with. "It bothered you to sleep with me." He thought back to the exact moment when she'd started to panic. "And the thought of opening up to me verbally."

She instantly put her head back on his shoulder, her body curling in upon itself until she easily fit on his lap. He wrapped his arms more firmly around her, trying to tell her that she was safe without using so many words. Finally, she spoke. "I don't do this."

"You said that last night. You don't sleep over."

"Yes, but I don't..." She waved her hand at nothing. "I don't do *any* of this. I don't sleep over. I don't ask my partners questions about their lives or past. We stick strictly to here and now, and then we move on with our separate lives."

A neat and tidy arrangement that avoided any chance of emotional attachment. He'd suspected that she kept an iron-clad hold of her relationships—if three times could be called a relationship—but this confirmed it. "You find it comforting to be able to put men safely in boxes where they can't hurt you."

"It's not about hurt. It's about boundaries." She hissed out a breath. "I don't have time for a relationship that might end up ruining my life."

He wasn't quite sure how she made that jump, though it most likely had to do with her parents. Not every relationship ended so dramatically, like it had when her mother woke up one morning and decided she didn't want her life anymore. Or, for that matter, his ex waking up after what he'd thought was the best sex of their lives and deciding to report him for domestic abuse. Z realized he was tightening his grip on Sara and forced himself to relax. Jennifer had chosen a safe word, and he would have lit himself on fire before he'd ignored her using it.

If she'd actually fucking used it.

Or, hell, if she'd shown any level of distress while he was flogging her. She'd begged—for more. It was only the next day, after he'd gone to work at the base, that she'd had buyer's remorse. He'd always suspected her sister was to blame, but he'd never been able to confirm one way or another because he'd been too busy watching his life fall apart around him, his name smeared through the dirt, his entire life ruined when she should have just *talked* to him. "I'm not your mother."

She flinched. "I don't know what—"

"No lies between us." He made an effort to temper his tone. "I've known Garrett long enough to know how things went down with your parents. It was shitty, really shitty, how your mom left."

She was quiet for the space of ten heartbeats, and finally relaxed against him. "I refuse to go through that kind of pain when it's so easy to avoid. You can't lose your heart in three dates—or fucks."

Maybe if she said it enough times, she'd actually believe it. But if she didn't care, she wouldn't have panicked—she would have ridden this shit out until it was over, thanked him, and moved on with her life. The fact that she was reacting this strongly—even negatively—meant he affected her as much as he was beginning to realize she affected him.

She was so damn courageous. Even when her life was spinning out of control, she managed to keep a sense of humor. And she challenged him, even as she submitted. He couldn't help but admire her, and wonder what else he would find out about her as they spent more time together.

He smoothed back her hair. "Your brothers seem to be doing just fine with their women."

"Sure." She huffed. "I know it's stupid, but I can't help feeling a little betrayed. Not by Garrett—he and Ridley have been in love since high school, even if they both did as much as possible to sabotage it for years. But Will…"

The other twin. Z had only met him once, but once was more than enough. The man had ice water in his veins, so the thought of him being swept away by a woman was stretching credibility. But apparently it'd happened. "I hear his woman is a force of nature."

"Penelope? Yeah, I guess she's okay." She sighed. "Sorry, I'm being catty. She *is* great. And Will has been as happy as I've ever seen him since they got together. It's just… It was always me and him, you know? He stayed when Garrett left. I used to joke about him and me being like our dad and Uncle Rodger with standing game nights once we hit middle age. And now he's got…her. He proposed. Did you know that? It's only a matter of time before they set a date and get married."

Marriage. The thought was nearly enough to make him break out in hives. He'd sworn that he'd never put a ring on another woman's finger after that nightmare finally ended. Z mentally shook himself. "I'm sorry."

"Don't be. I guess it was kind of silly to think they'd go their entire lives without settling down. I just… They moved out, you know? Not too long after my mom left they were both in their own places. I saw the damage it did to my father, how hard it was for him to pick up the pieces. He almost lost his job because he could barely get up the energy to go to work, and I basically had to fend for myself."

Hearing that made him want to wrap her up and protect her. She didn't need it. She'd come through—bringing her father with her, if his current happiness was any indication—and prospered. But it couldn't be more obvious that, despite everything she'd done to succeed, she still wore the scars. "Sara."

She lifted her head and looked at him. "Yeah?"

"I won't make you sleep next to me again if you don't want to."

Chapter Eleven

Sara couldn't believe she was telling him some of this stuff—she hadn't even been able to tell Ridley her feelings about Will because her friend was so jazzed up on her own happiness. And she *was* happy for her brothers. But it still stung.

Z hadn't called her a monster or told her that she was selfish for feeling this way. And now he was offering to take away one of the things that had spooked her in the first place. She bit her lip. Now that she'd calmed down a little, it seemed kind of ridiculous for her to react so strongly in the first place. "I feel a little silly for freaking out."

"Don't. You're entitled to feel the way you do, regardless of the cause." He gripped the back of her neck, the feeling of his hand more a comfort than she ever could have anticipated. "But you *will* talk to me about it next time, instead of trying to run."

Next time.

More talking.

The thought should panic her even more, but there was something steady about Z that settled her in spite of herself. He was a rock—if one that liked to toss her around and beat her ass and make her come... She shifted, half-surprised at how quickly things had gone from fear to heat. She licked her lips. "Okay."

"Now, be honest with me—do you want this to stop?" He asked it without anything in his tone condemning her decision one way or another. If she said she never wanted him to touch her again, he'd back off and they'd spend the rest of this exile...what? Warily? Awkwardly? Fighting every second to keep from touching each other? All of the above?

Or she could let go of her fear and grab this thing with both hands and ride it out to its conclusion.

When she thought of it that way, there wasn't much of a choice. As much as she hated the idea of letting him in enough to really hurt her, she hated the idea of ending this now even more. She dredged up what remained of her courage. "I don't want this to stop... Sir."

His green eyes bored into hers, demanding the truth. "Are you sure?"

"I'm sure."

Z sat back and took off his necklace. It was a small golden circle with a compass rose over the top, the directions holding their normal positions—north on top, south on bottom, east and west on either side. He set it over her head. "I don't have a collar, but this will do for the time being." He twisted the chain, tightening it ever so slightly around her throat. "If it gets to be too much, or you start to panic, *tell me*. Do you understand?"

She swallowed hard. "Yes, Sir."

"Good girl." He kissed her, a quick brushing of the lips. "Now, let's see about some food."

Just like that, they were back on familiar territory. He let her climb to her feet and he paused to pull on a pair of pants. She started to reach for her robe, but a sharp look from him had her leaving it on the floor. Naked it was. Sara had always been comfortable in her own skin, but there was definitely something erotic about being naked while he was partially dressed, especially when she could feel his gaze on her every step down the hall and stairs. In the kitchen, she opened the fridge and shivered when a blast of cold air hit the front of her body. "I can make bacon, but I'm not doing it naked."

A chuckle had her turning to find him dangling an apron from one finger. It was frilly and would barely cover her chest, but she still took it and tied it on with a grin. "Pervert."

"I like to have my cake and eat it, too." His gaze coasted down her body, leaving no illusions to what he considered cake. She resisted the urge to fan herself and set about putting breakfast together.

It was a hot mess.

She was so distracted with Z sitting at the island, watching her, that she burnt the bacon to a crisp, broke all the egg yolks, and over-salted the hash browns. If there were anything edible on the two plates she made up, she would be surprised. But she still set it in front of him, partially because she was curious to see what he'd do.

He poked the bacon, and snorted when it crumbled. "Do I make you nervous, sweetheart?"

Was that a joke? Of course he made her nervous. It was like being in a room with a tiger, not sure if he was going to cozy up to her or maul her... Though she'd be okay with both options, it didn't make for a relaxing morning, either way. He watched her like he wanted an honest answer, so she shrugged. "Only mostly."

"You weren't nervous last night."

Things felt different now that she'd gone and spilled all her issues all over him. And he hadn't blinked or paused or backed away. It felt like something had shifted inside her, and she wasn't sure she liked the new arrangement. She smoothed a hand over the ridiculous apron. "No, I wasn't."

He snagged her wrist, pulling her to stand between his legs. "I like that I make you a little nervous."

"Sadist."

"Nah." He laughed, a big grin settling on his face. It was like night and day. Before he'd been devastatingly attractive. Now? Now, he was heartbreaking. Because there was something like happiness in those pale green eyes, the same happiness that mirrored what seemed to course through her very veins when she was around him. It didn't make any sense. Two people couldn't reach anything beyond lust in such a short time, but…

It didn't matter. She liked seeing him smile, so she'd work to get that expression on his face as often as she possibly could. Now was as good a time to start as any. Sara framed his face with her hands and pressed a quick kiss to his lips. "Thank you."

"For?"

"For making me talk. I didn't realize how much I needed it until everything was all out there." It still didn't feel completely natural to open up to him—to anyone—about this sort of thing, but he'd heard her out and hadn't called her a selfish bitch—even though she'd deserved it. It had settled something deep inside her, like a jagged little piece of her soul that had been scraping at her heart ever since Will and Penelope got together had been sanded to smoothness.

Her therapist would have a field day with that.

...

There were a whole hell of a lot of thoughts dancing across Sara's face. She'd taken a leap earlier, and Z fully planned on rewarding the display of trust. But for now, he wanted to keep things light. He poked at the charred mess on his plate. "Is this a test to see how bad I feel about pushing you so hard last night?"

She laughed, that wonderfully free sound that he loved so much. "Maybe. Is it working?"

"Consider me sufficiently repentant." He pressed a kiss to her bare shoulder and stood. "But I think cold cereal would be a safer bet."

"Chicken."

He turned to find her emptying both plates into the garbage. "That makes two of us."

"Sure does. Now sit your fine ass down. I think my nervousness has passed enough that we don't have to soldier through cold cereal." She said it like bran flakes was on the same level as dog food.

"God forbid." He leaned against the counter and watched her get to work, pointedly ignoring him as she started another helping of bacon. "Who taught you to cook?"

"Believe it or not, it was Uncle Rodger." She smiled, her gaze going distant as she broke eggs into a bowl. "My... My mother took care of that kind of thing before she left, and she never let anyone in the kitchen to help. So after she was gone it was a mess. We ate a truly terrifying amount of fast food and pizza. Then one day, right before the twins graduated, Uncle Rodger showed up. He only came around on the weekends, since he had his business to run, but he managed to impart a lot of knowledge to all three of us."

"He sounds like a remarkable man."

"He is." She shot a guilty look over her shoulder. "I mean, I love my dad. A lot. But my uncle is as unmovable as a rock. Even when he wasn't around, I knew he was just a phone call away. It helped."

He watched her for a few minutes longer, comparing this new information with what he knew of her. "You never called, did you?"

Sara laughed. "Not once."

That made sense. From everything he'd seen, she was fiercely independent, and she looked up to Rodger in a big way. It was understandable that she wouldn't want to show him weakness, whether it was to avoid disappointing him, or to try to live up to his example. "But you called your brothers." Surely *someone* was there to help her when she got into trouble.

"Only when there was no other option." She stirred the eggs. "But we all survived and turned into mostly normal functioning adults, so I guess it worked out just fine." Toast was once against laid out on a pan, buttered, and put in the still-warm oven. "What about you? Any family missing you when you're traipsing all over the world?"

"No." He realized how abrupt the word sounded and tried to soften it. "My parents have been gone a long time, and I have no siblings."

"So the guys in your group are like a family, huh?"

He shot her a surprised look that she didn't catch because she was flipping the bacon. He'd never said it aloud, but he'd definitely come to see his men as brothers, of sorts. Garrett especially. It was part of the reason why he went to great lengths to make sure they didn't have to shoulder any more shit than strictly necessary.

Not if he could shoulder it for them.

"That's not a bad comparison." He shouldn't be surprised by her observation—she'd already proven herself to be incredibly intelligent—but it was strange to hear it.

"I have my moments." The oven dinged and she turned with a flourish. "Now, sit down for real. Allow your obedient sub to serve you an edible breakfast."

"Obedient sub. I don't think you know the meaning of the words." He sat, enjoying the mischievous grin she wore as she placed the plate before him with overdone extravagance. "You *definitely* don't know the meaning of the word."

"You're probably right." She grabbed her plate.

Z watched her out of the corner of his eye as he ate. It was interesting that she seemed to open up in the kitchen—at least after she got over the initial shakiness from earlier this morning. But this room, much like the pool area, was a place where she was totally and completely comfortable.

Actually, that wasn't correct, either.

She'd been fine in her room. The *only* place where things had been less than open was in *his* bedroom. His territory. That was when she'd gone on the defensive. Interesting.

He enjoyed the comfortable silence until she'd once again cleared the plates. "You don't have to do that."

"It's two plates, not a Thanksgiving feast." She shrugged

with a little smile. "I never do dishes for family dinners."

God, he loved the way her grin lit up her whole face. Z held out a hand. "Come here."

She immediately crossed to him and let him pull her closer. "See, I'm being obedient. And submissive."

Z snorted and lifted her onto the kitchen island, situating her so that her legs fell on either side of him. "You can always talk to me."

"I thought that's what we were just doing."

He lightly smacked her thigh. "Brat." He needed her to understand, though, so he didn't touch her anywhere else. "I meant about earlier. It's important to me that I know where your boundaries are. I might be an ass, but I don't want to traumatize you."

"I know." She tilted her head down so that her hair fell to partially cover her face. "And I do feel better—obviously. Even if I wanted to do…ill advised things when you hauled me back into your room."

"Like hit me again." He slid a hand beneath the apron, cupping her between her legs. "You know what happens if you do."

"Yes, Sir." It was barely more than a sigh.

As much as he wanted to keep talking, he didn't want to press her too hard. What had felt like lancing a wound could all too easily turn into a whole new problem if he wasn't careful. Beyond that, she didn't regret last night, which meant he could change directions and push her more physically while she got used to the new emotional closeness. It was a common tactic his team had deployed time and again—albeit with a different end goal. Harry an enemy, pushing them one way, and then circling around to strike where they least expected. It kept the opponent off center and uncertain—which is where he needed Sara to be until she realized he wasn't going anywhere.

He wasn't sure when he'd made that decision. He didn't deserve a woman like her—that much was for damn sure. But he didn't care about that shit right now. It was selfish and might be plain wrong, but it was becoming clearer with each passing hour that he wanted her in a way that had nothing to do with sex.

So he meant to have her.

"Would you like your reward, sweetheart?" He shifted his hand, leisurely exploring her pussy as he watched her face.

"Definitely." She nodded. "Yes, Sir."

"Good. Because I'm starving." He guided her so she was leaning back, resting on her elbows, and looking down her body at him. Her breasts strained against the apron, to the point where one sharp tug would reveal her nipples. With the lace, it created a strange combination of erotic and wholesome.

It made him so hard, he could barely see straight.

Z spread her legs even wider and used his free hand to push up the bottom of the apron. She was so wet, his fingers glistened when he withdrew them. *Fuck.* He pulled her to the very edge of the counter and dragged his tongue over her center. Her cry was music to his ears, and he wasted no time tasting every inch of her heated flesh—except her clit. "You taste so fucking good—better than breakfast, and sure as fuck better than whatever you were burning in the pan earlier."

Her laugh was strangled. "Thank you, Sir."

He moved up to suck her clit into his mouth, working her for a few seconds before he reluctantly sat back. As much as he wanted to spend more time with his mouth on her, he had something else in mind. He pinned her hips down with his hands, using his thumbs to stroke her pussy, following the same wandering path his tongue had just taken. "There's something I want to know."

"Yes, Sir?"

"You have no problem taking what you want." He circled her clit once, twice, before moving away. Her chest heaved with each breath, and her hips would have been rising to meet him if he wasn't holding them in place. "But there's something you've never done that you always wanted to."

"What makes you…think that…?" She moaned, letting her body fully rest on the counter and touching her breasts. "Sir?"

"Stop that. Hands behind your neck." He waited for her to obey before he started stroking her again. "Because I'm beginning to know you, sweetheart. You've kept something back—you always do. Tell me." He pushed a finger into her, but withdrew it before she could truly enjoy the penetration. "Tell me, or you won't come today."

Her eyes flew open. "You wouldn't."

"Are you willing to call my bluff and find out?" He wouldn't enjoy doing it…much…but he sure as fuck wasn't bluffing. "Tell me."

"People watching." She gasped it out. "I got off on knowing you could see me, but couldn't touch. I want to be fucked where people can do the same."

He paused. "You're a regular at Serve."

"No, I'm not. I slip in there when there's no chance of the

trauma of seeing my brothers in compromising positions."

He could see why she wouldn't have gone for a true extrovert scene. Even hedging her bets with the twins being occupied elsewhere, there was still a chance they could show up. Well, that was a worry he could remove for the time being.

He stood and undid his pants, freeing his cock. "You want me to fuck you where anyone can see." He grabbed one of the condoms from the cargo pocket and put it on while she watched. "They'll see this pretty pussy." He jerked her even further off the edge of the counter and shoved into her. "They'll be so fucking jealous of my cock, they'll lose their damn minds." He kept going, the force of his thrusts making her breasts bounce. The sight of his dark cock disappearing into her made him wild, desperate for more, even if he wasn't exactly sure what the *more* was he wanted. "They can't have it, Sara. They can't have *you*. You're mine."

She arched off the counter as she came, her cry loud enough that it was a wonder the windows didn't shake. He drew her to him, kissing her as he finished, emptying himself inside her. In the back of his mind, a voice whispered, *This is two*. Even as sure as he wanted to be of Sara, there was still the question of if she'd go past her limit of three times.

Because he wasn't sure he wanted to let her go.

Chapter Twelve

Once they could walk again, Z dragged Sara upstairs for a shower. She half-expected him to take her again in the big walk-in that was half the size of her apartment, but he merely kissed her and then set about washing himself off. She liked that, liked that he didn't feel the need to be all over her or, God forbid, washing her hair. Plus, with him across the space, she got plenty of opportunity to eye-fuck the hell out of him. "You, Sir, are gorgeous."

His dark laugh was the only answer she got. All too soon, it was over and he was wrapping her in a fluffy white towel. She sat on the bed and watched him get dressed, wondering at the scars that peppered his body. One on his lower side was clearly a bullet wound—Garrett had a similar one on his shoulder—but the others were harder to pinpoint.

"Ask."

She jumped. "It's nothing."

"Sara, you're entitled to questions."

She had half a million when it came to Z. He was an enigma at best, one she'd come to know biblically, but their conversations had only offered glimpses of the man behind the Dom. Wanting that sort of thing wasn't normally something she suffered from—she might be twice as curious as a cat, but not about the men she slept with. He was different, though. *This* was different.

And if she thought about that too hard, it was going to scare the shit out of her. She fully intended to ask about his scars, but when she opened her mouth, that wasn't what came out. "Why don't you date?"

His eyebrows shot up. "*What?*"

"I know men are different from women, but Garrett said you never date. Ever. I'd like to know why."

He hesitated, and she had the sudden thought that he was considering lying to her. It stung a lot more than it should have, but she folded her hands and waited. If he lied, then there wasn't a damn thing she could do about it. It would be a betrayal of the trust he seemed to value so highly, but she wasn't going to condemn him for *thinking* about lying.

God, she hoped he told the truth.

Finally, he crossed to sit on the bed next to her, but far enough away that he clearly didn't want to be touched. She resented that distance between them, even as she called herself a fool for doing so. "You know I value control. The first time I've lost it in seven years is because of you."

Was that supposed to be a compliment or an insult?

He still wouldn't look at her. "I got married while I was in the Army. I was young and stupid and thought putting a ring on her finger really meant for better or worse. But there was part of me I never really let go with her and she could tell. We used to fight." He sighed. "Fuck, we fought like you wouldn't believe. So two years in, I finally let that part of myself off the leash."

He spoke so calmly, with each word carefully set between them as if something would shatter if he let any emotion in. It broke her heart. "You mean kinky stuff." Like what they'd been doing since they met. Really, compared to some of the Doms she knew, Z hadn't gotten even *close* to crossing any lines with his pain play. Hell, all he'd done was spank her. Her body warmed at the thought, and she silently told it to pipe the fuck down. Now wasn't the time to get all hot and bothered.

"Yeah. We talked beforehand. She said she was good with it. Even during, I kept checking on her and she was *fine*." His voice rose, and he forced it back down. "I went to work the next morning, still thinking everything was okay—right up until the base cops showed up."

She blinked, sure she'd heard him wrong, but he didn't correct himself. "*Cops?*"

He kept going like he hadn't heard her. "I lost everything. She filed a restraining order and left me. I was dishonorably discharged. Hell, the only reason I didn't see jail time was because my lawyer was a goddamn pit bull."

She couldn't just sit there and pretend like the memories weren't hurting both of them. What kind of woman did that to a man she'd married? Safe words were there for a reason—they were sacred within the BDSM community, and she'd already seen how perceptive Z was. He wouldn't have kept going if his wife was in distress, even if she'd been too stubborn or stupid to safe out. Sara crawled to him and wrapped her arms around him, pressing her body against his back. "I'm so sorry."

"The worst part was how my friends turned on me. Suddenly I was a wife beater and a piece of shit." He shook a little, and her heart cracked open even further. She hugged him tighter, not sure if he noticed at all.

"No one knows."

She lifted her head. "What?"

"No one. Not my team, not your brother, no one. Except now you." He shrugged. "It's a matter of public record, but they came to me when I already had a reputation for getting the job done in the private sector."

It was tempting to let it go, but she couldn't. "Z."

"Yeah?"

"I don't know about the rest of your team, but Garrett would never take a job with someone he hadn't checked out. Our family isn't exactly big on trust." The understatement of the century.

"You're wrong."

She wasn't, but she couldn't confirm without asking Garrett. If it comforted Z to think that no one knew about his past, then she'd let him go on thinking that—for now. But anyone with half a brain who got a hold of the police reports would see the truth. Especially someone like her brother, who actively practiced BDSM.

Her mind kept going back to the betrayal he had to have felt when he realized what was happening. He'd basically bared a secret part of himself to his wife and she'd shit all over it. It made Sara want to punch something.

But that response wouldn't do a damn thing to help him now, so many years later. Plus, from how tense his body was, she was pretty sure he was prepared for her to reject him out of hand after hearing the truth. For being such an observant man, his personal issues gave him a serious blind spot. She couldn't help with that. But she *could* reassure him here and now.

So she kissed the back of his neck. "I'm sorry. You deserved better."

...

Z had been prepared for Sara to reel back and look at him with disgust when she learned about his past. But here she was, comforting him like *he* was the victim. He turned to face her. "I don't think you understand. I almost went to jail for beating my wife."

"A beating she asked you for. Literally asked you for." Her blue eyes held none of the judgment he'd seen in so many. "Unless I'm wrong? She *did* want this, didn't she? And you explained to her what you wanted and expected, just like you did with me, right?"

"Yes," he said reluctantly.

"I thought so." She kissed his forehead. "She asked for something she really didn't want, which was something you should have seen. But that doesn't mean you deserved what happened." She kissed both corners of his mouth. "No one deserves that. And if I thought for a second that you actually abused your wife, we wouldn't still be having this conversation. Understand?"

Surely it couldn't be that simple. "I don't think *you* understand."

"I understand that I feel more alive when you're touching me than I have in a very long time." She moved down to his jaw. "I love the spanking that you gave me. And I love the way you talk to me." The hollow of his throat. "I understand that I can't get enough of you, even if that scares me. I want to kneel at your feet and call you, 'Sir.'"

He shuddered at the picture she painted. "I don't deserve you."

"Probably not." She laughed against his skin. "But you have me." The silent *for now* hung between them.

The doorbell rang, and Z was off the bed and had Sara halfway to the bathroom before he fully registered the sound. He guided her the rest of the way in, his heart beating too hard. "Stay here until I come for you. Your brother says you know how to shoot—there's a gun in the bottom drawer. Anyone besides me comes through this door, you use it."

"Wait—"

He left the bathroom, shutting the door behind him, and then did the same with the bedroom door. Part of the reason he'd been glad Rodger picked a house this size was the ability for Sara to hide long enough for him to eliminate a threat.

Or for reinforcements to show up.

Speaking of... He should have gotten some kind of warning. Z patted his pockets, coming up empty, and cursed. Where the fuck was his phone? He paused to step into another room and retrieve a gun he'd slipped beneath the mattress and then headed down the stairs, alert and ready for any attack.

The doorbell rang again, ratcheting up his nerves. He moved in a half-crouch to the side room where he could see the front entryway. A FedEx truck was parked outside, a tiny woman, holding a massive box, standing at the door, her foot tapping. She didn't look like some hardcore assassin, but looks could be deceiving.

Either way, she didn't appear to be leaving anytime soon.

He kept the gun drawn and walked into the foyer and opened the door, ready for any kind of attack. Instead, she just huffed an impatient breath and set the box on the front doorstep. Then she shoved a little machine at him. "Finally. Sign here."

Feeling increasingly idiotic, he signed and watched her walk back to her truck and drive away. Then his attention landed on the package itself. Just because the delivery woman wasn't an enemy didn't mean the danger had passed. He carefully set the gun on the decorative table and pulled a knife from his pocket. A quick flick of his wrist split the tape and he pulled back the cardboard flaps. "What. The. Fuck?"

"What is it?"

Z spun around. "You're supposed to stay put until I come get you."

"And leave you to get taken out by an army of FedEx employees? No way." She hurried down the rest of the stairs, and it was only then that he noticed his gun in her hands. She handled it like a pro, but that made sense—between Rodger and Garrett, she had plenty of men in her life determined to ensure she could protect herself.

The fact that she was still naked seemed to be lost on her.

Sara peeked into the box and laughed. "Oh my God. She didn't!" She set her gun next to his and bent over, giving him a heart-stopping view of her ass before she rose, dangling a blindfold from her finger. Another dive brought up a flogger. "She really went all out."

"Who?" He couldn't take his gaze away from the flogger, his mind only too happy to supply the images of Sara tied down, her skin red from his strikes, her begging filling his ears. He turned away, taking a deep breath to regain control. "We need to get the box inside."

"Sure thing." She dragged it into the house and kicked the door shut. "Now we can have some real fun."

What the fuck was he going to do with this woman? If Z's life had taught him anything, it was that if something seemed too good to be true, it most likely was. And every single damn thing about Sara Reaver was exactly that. It was enough to make him wonder when the other shoe was going to drop.

Chapter Thirteen

Before Sara could really dig into the goodies Ridley had sent, Z muttered something about checking in with his men and disappeared. Thirty minutes went by and she finally decided that she was going to have to entertain herself for a while. The poolroom was delightfully warm, the winter sunlight streaking in through the glass.

She dove in and swam a few laps. The feeling of her naked body cutting through the water had never felt so erotic, but then, she didn't spend a lot of time skinny-dipping. It was going to be a damn shame when she had to go back to reality and the pool at her gym.

Her gym that she hadn't spent nearly enough time at in recent weeks, if the fatigue she felt was anything to judge by. She used to swim a few miles a day, but now she was barely over one and failing fast. She'd let a hell of a lot go while she was tracking down evidence of Nord's parking garage hookup. It had become personal, which by now was something she knew better than to let happen. Business was supposed to be business. She had to care—if she didn't, she'd be shitty at her job. But it was a fine line between caring and becoming obsessed—a fine line she'd definitely crossed.

She'd screwed up. Sara swam to the shallow end and walked out of the pool, pausing to squeeze the water of out her hair. She could admit that now, even if she hadn't been able to a few days ago. If she hadn't been so focused on bringing Nord down, she would have noticed the heat she was attracting—would have actually backed off when Uncle Rodger ordered her to—instead of charging blindly ahead. He was rarely wrong, and this time was no exception. She was going to have to call and apologize—and definitely buy him some of the expensive scotch he favored when this was all over.

That could wait, though. She'd been sent here to stay out of their way, and calling every few minutes wasn't going to prove that she could follow orders. She sat on one of the lounge chairs situated around the edge of the pool and laid back. In the meantime, she was going to enjoy the sun and warmth and relax for a little bit.

She'd found a library in her wanderings, and picked up the romance novel she'd decided on. It was old enough to have a shiny cover with a man who could have passed for Fabio on it. Though she hadn't expected to enjoy it, a few pages in, she got sucked into the torrid affair between the Duke of somewhere she'd never heard of and the orphan virgin heroine.

She wasn't aware of time passing, so she jumped when lightning flashed above her, followed by thunder so loud she *swore* the glass shook in response. Even knowing she probably had nothing to worry about, she still dropped the book and moved away from the pool. Some habits were too ingrained to fight—if there was a storm, you stayed the hell away from any body of water.

She didn't go far, though, because the lightning flashed again, a gorgeous forking across the sky. Rain hit the roof in sheets, the sound almost as loud as the thunder. They had storms in the city, of course, but it felt different here, with only the ceiling of glass between her and the elements. Wilder. She had the insane urge to slip outside and dance in the rain, and only the knowledge that it'd be freezing and miserable kept her rooted in place.

She felt him come in behind her, though that should have been impossible. But sometime in the last three days, her body had become so attuned to Z's that she wasn't the least bit surprised when he slipped his arms around her waist and rested his chin on the top of her head. "Fierce storm tonight."

"I think it's beautiful."

The power flickered and went out, leaving them bathed in darkness. She jumped, smacking her head into Z's chin. "Ouch."

"Come on." He took her hand and led her into the house. It was like a completely different place in the dark, furniture rearing out, threatening to smack into her legs with every step. But he led her unerringly around it, moving from one room to the next until she felt cool tile beneath her bare feet. A flash of lightning showed what she'd suspected—the kitchen.

"I need to learn how to do that." She took a cautious step forward and touched the shadow that resolved itself into the island.

"Do what?" His voice echoed slightly.

"Memorize a place well enough to be able to move through it in the dark. That's got to be a useful skill." Her job took her into some sketchy places, and it couldn't hurt to be able to move quietly without bringing attention to herself.

"Are you planning on breaking into someone's house?"

She grinned. "I didn't say that."

"You were thinking it." He moved next to her and set things on the island with a thump. A few seconds later, a match struck, lighting up the space between them. He wasted no time in lighting the thick white candles he'd found somewhere. "Are you hungry?"

"Starving." She hadn't eaten since that morning. She took one of the candles and walked over to grab sandwich stuff from the shelves. "Peanut butter and jelly okay?"

"Works for me."

She went about putting them together—one for her, two for Z—while he watched her. She glanced up and had to make an effort not to sigh at the way the candlelight played along his dark skin and killer cheekbones. He was gorgeous under normal circumstances, but this made her think back to a time before electricity and polite society, where the strong and feral ruled. She suspected he'd be perfectly at home hunting with bows and arrows and celebrating a successful kill around a campfire with a woman on one side and a brood of children on the other.

Whoa. That was enough of *that*.

They ate in silence, her mind still reeling from that unexpected turn. Sara didn't want kids. No, that wasn't strictly true. She didn't mind children—in theory. They were cute and cuddly and totally life changing. And, though her childhood had been pretty good as such things went, there was the whole boatload of abandonment issues she now carted around to consider. She didn't want to pass those along. Beyond that, she'd probably be a shitty parent. No, no kids for her.

She glanced up to find Z watching her. He held out his hand. "Come."

Well, *that* she could get on board with.

• • •

Z had spent the day doing his damnedest not to be rattled. He'd never told anyone what happened with his ex, but he'd been prepared for Sara to do anything but accept him wholeheartedly. All it did was reinforce his growing certainty that he had to convince her to stay. Easier said than done. If he tried to force the issue or bully her, submissive or not, she'd dig in her heels and tell him to get lost. No, he'd have to wrap her up so tightly that she never wanted to be let go. And *that* would be a challenge he relished.

He blew out all but two candles and led her upstairs. While she'd been relaxing by the pool, he'd hauled up the box of toys Ridley sent—which still wigged him out a bit—and unpacked them. They walked into the room he'd set up and he pointed at the bed. "Sit."

"Yes, Sir." She woofed and dropped primly onto the edge of the mattress.

He turned away so she wouldn't see his smile and went about lighting the candles he'd arranged on the dresser. There were half a dozen of them in a rainbow of colors—and he fully intended to use them all tonight. He moved back to the bed and couldn't resist kissing her. That mouth, so quick to quirk into humor, was far more tempting than the best kind of alcohol. Her tongue swiped his, and she moaned when he drew back. "Onto the bed."

She crawled backwards and lifted her arms over her head and spread her legs, already knowing how he wanted her positioned. He picked up the cuffs from the dresser and attached her ankles to the footboard, before circling around to do the same to her wrists. "Tell me your safe word."

"Wolfman."

"Use it if you have to."

"I won't have to." Her expression was so tender and full of trust that something in his chest split wide open.

Fighting to keep some modicum of control, he grabbed the blindfold and slipped it over her eyes. "You are beautiful, sweetheart. Your body is a canvas that begs for my marks."

"Yes, Sir."

Nothing but desire in her tone—desire and expectation. He leaned over and took her closest nipple into his mouth, kissing it the same way he'd kissed her mouth earlier. When she gasped, he moved to the other breast. He needed her desperate before he started in on the next step. He moved around the bed to settle between her legs, taking his time tasting her, circling her clit with his tongue. Her body shook with pleasure, teetering on the edge of orgasm.

It was only then that he lifted his head and pushed to his feet. She cried out, "Sir, *please*."

"Not yet." He checked the candles. They were sufficiently burned down, each containing a small pool of wax in the center. "Tell me your favorite color."

She hesitated, her body tensing. "Blue."

"Hmmm." He picked up the blue candle. "Do you trust me?"

"Yes, Sir." No hesitation this time.

Fuck, did this woman know what she did to him? He'd never known how much he needed that unquestioning trust until she submitted like this. "Good girl." He tipped the candle, letting a drop of wax fall onto her sternum.

She hissed out a breath, arching into the mattress. He waited, but she didn't use her safe word, so he dribbled a bit more wax onto her skin, up the curve of her breast, stopping just short of her nipple. She squirmed and bit her lip, but she stayed silent.

It would be easier if he could see her eyes, but he wanted her tense and alert and uncertain of where the next contact would come from. Which meant he needed verbal confirmation that she was fine. He *couldn't* lose her like he lost Jennifer. "Sara?"

"I'm fine, Sir." She gave a shaky laugh. "Better than fine."

A part of him wondered if she was lying to please him... but Sara knew better. And trust had to go both ways. If he didn't trust her to be honest with him, then he had no business playing these kinds of games with her. "Good." The next bit of wax landed on her nipple, and she cried out.

This time, he kept going. Z repeated the line up her other breast and around her nipple, and then moved down her stomach, stopping just short of her belly button. The candles were created specifically for this purpose—burning at a lesser temperature than normal candles, to remove the chance of actual injury—but her pale skin was still red around the edges of the wax. He liked it. Fuck, he more than liked it.

He set the blue candle aside and considered. Green was the next logical choice. So he used that color wax to draw circles around her stomach and up the outside curve of her breasts, and then down the center again, thickening the lines he'd started with the blue. She shook with each drip of wax against her skin, but he recognized the way her hips twisted.

Little Sara Reaver was loving this as much as he was.

This time he chose the red candle. "Brace yourself."

"What—*oh my God*."

He dropped a stream across the sensitive bare skin above her pussy, and the wax ran down the dips created by her pelvic bone, creating a frame that he found he liked very much. He used his free hand to stroke her, just once, finding her even more wet than she'd been under his tongue. "You love this."

"Fuck yes, Sir."

"Good." He finished covering her nipples with the red wax, enjoying her cries. Next it was the black, the white, and the yellow, until she was a myriad of colors. Then he sat back to let it completely harden. It wouldn't take long, but he liked watching her, seeing his handiwork and knowing her reactions were a result of *his* actions.

He liked that a whole hell of a lot.

Chapter Fourteen

Sara had never thought her body could feel so over-sensitized. The wax had burned, but now that it hardened, the sensation of it resisting her movements only made her hotter. It was like a strange form of bondage that she could break through if she really tried…but she totally didn't want to.

Z dragged the blindfold off, leaving her blinking in the low light. She immediately looked down her body, and gasped at the pretty pattern of mixed colors covering her. "Wow."

"I'm not done, yet." He uncuffed her, and helped her up without dislodging too much of the wax. She let him maneuver her to the end of the bed, and stood silently watching as he shoved off his pants and rolled on a condom. He sat at the edge of the mattress, nearly in the exact spot she'd taken when they came in earlier. He held out his hand in silent command and she took it. But when she went to straddle him, he turned her around and lifted her onto his lap, using his legs to keep hers spread wide. He took her chin and lifted it. "Look."

There was a freestanding mirror, similar to the one in her bedroom, directly across from them. The candlelight glinted off her body as he lowered her onto his cock, the angle perfect to see every inch disappear inside her. The contrast of their skin was only accented by the wax, and she couldn't take her eyes off their reflection as he guided her to ride him in long, slow strokes.

He coasted his hands up her body, making the wax crumble and flake away, leaving her skin unbelievably sensitized. Z pinched her nipples, and fire shot through her veins, making her gasp. So, of course, the bastard did it again. While one hand kept up that motion, the other skated down her stomach to stroke her clit. He left the wax framing her pussy alone, and the picture they created? Yeah, it was enough to send her to the edge. "Z, I—"

"Come. I've got you." He squeezed her clit, his green eyes intent on her face in the mirror as her body came apart around him. Sara twisted around, and he met her halfway, kissing her as the second wave rolled over her. She barely had time to take a breath before he was up and turning, pressing her facedown onto the bed and thrusting into her from behind. She braced herself as best she could, but she had no illusions—Z held all the control.

"Touch yourself. Now."

She reached between her legs, her clit already so sensitive that it took the barest touch to bring her over the edge again, driven by the man behind her, filling her with his cock. She screamed into the comforter, vaguely aware of Z's strokes becoming less controlled and more savage. He came with a curse, his fingers digging into her hipbones hard enough that she was sure she'd wear his marks tomorrow.

Good.

He withdrew from her and stood, pulling her up with him. "Shower." He took one of the candles with them into the bathroom and frowned. "It's going to be cold, but there's no help for it. Hold on." She waited, still dazed, while he turned on the water and slipped beneath it with a curse that had her laughing…until he dragged her in behind him.

The cold was a shock her to system, and she cursed just as loudly as he had, while he scrubbed her down in quick, efficient swipes. Less than a minute later, she was as clean she was going to get, and he shut off the shower. Sara squeezed the water from her hair. "Sadist."

"You love it."

There was that word again. She said it nearly as often as he did, but it made her stomach twist uncomfortably. Because it was something she went out of her way not to use casually—until now. "Yeah."

He wrapped a towel around her and then another around himself. It was horribly domestic, and she lapped it up like it was something she'd been missing all her life. Maybe she had. She stopped in the doorway back to the bedroom and took in the wax that seemed to cover every surface of the bed and floor. "Maybe we should try a different room."

"Your room."

It was a calculated move. Even with her head practically floating off her shoulders from remembered pleasure, she knew that. He could have picked any of the other half a dozen rooms on this side of the house. They were all empty and more than big enough for their purpose. But he was leading her to the room she'd claimed for her own—the one that was as close to her own territory as she could possibly get in a house that wasn't hers.

He was taking it into account and trying to make her as comfortable as she could be. Her chest warmed at the realization. Z wouldn't put this amount of thought into something if he didn't really want her to be okay with sleeping next to him.

It struck her that there was no reason for them to share a bed tonight. That had been time number three, which meant this thing between them had reached its predetermined expiration date. Sara hugged the towel to her chest, cold in a way that had nothing to do with the water. If she were smart, she'd say it now, lay it out there, and retreat. He'd agreed to it, the same as she had.

She looked up to find him watching her, seeing too much. "Do you want me to find another room?"

He knew. Of course he knew. He could count, after all.

All she had to do was say yes, and he'd do just that. He didn't look like he *wanted* to, but he would. The question that remained was... Did *she* want him to sleep somewhere else?

No. The answer came almost before she'd finished the question. If he wasn't going to call her on the three times thing, then maybe she could relax the rule. *I'm not ready for this to end.* "No."

His smile was a reward in and of itself. "Good."

She caught herself relaxing, but didn't try to fight it. This day was going too well to ruin it by bringing her issues into it. Eventually they'd have to talk about it, but if he wasn't going to push her, she wasn't going to. All she wanted was to enjoy this time with this man.

Once in her room, he pulled her onto the bed and beneath the covers. She tensed for a moment, instinct fighting against relaxing in his arms, but finally her mind prevailed and her body followed. She turned in his arms, draped a leg over his waist, and buried her nose in the crook of his neck. He smelled like the outdoors—fresh and clean—and his body heat warmed her despite the power still being out. Words came, words she'd had no intention of ever voicing. But, just like before, it was all too easy to say them to Z. "I like you."

He went still, his chest barely rising and falling. "I like you, too, Sara."

It was hard to speak, harder than she could have imagined. "Once this is over—I mean, once it's safe to go back to the city—would you…" She took a deep breath and just rushed through the last bit. "Do you want to go out?"

"Date you?"

"Yes." The word was barely more than a whisper, and she had to fight the completely irrational urge to immediately take it back.

His arms tightened around her. "I'd like nothing more."

She'd hoped he'd say that, but hearing it still reassured her. They could do this. They could take it one step at a time and go slow, and work through both their issues as things arose. It didn't have to be scary or the end of the world that they had sex more than three times. Everything was going to be okay. It didn't have to end.

...

Z opened his eyes to find himself alone in Sara's bed. He waited, but she didn't reappear, and the bathroom seemed uninhabited, so he climbed out of bed. It took a grand total of five seconds to figure out where she'd gone. He stood in the window and watched her swim. It was different than it had been yesterday—she hadn't run from him, so much as run to the water. He could respect that.

A quick flip of the light switch told him the power had come on sometime during the night, so he went downstairs to brew some coffee. Once he had two mugs full, he made his way to the pool. Sara floated face up, her eyes closed and her hair a cloud around her head like some sort of siren from legend. She sure as fuck was tempting enough to alter his course, though he hoped like hell he wasn't heading for disaster.

She opened her eyes. "I couldn't sleep and didn't want to wake you."

"You didn't." Which spoke volumes. Normally, he knew the second someone walked into or out of a room he was in, even when asleep, but he'd never noticed she was gone. He held up the mugs. "I brought coffee."

"Yes, please." She climbed out of the pool and walked over to grab a towel. "How'd you sleep?"

"Good." Better than he could have expected. He took a drink of his coffee and watched her, searching for signs that she was regretful or less than comfortable. None of the indicators were there. In fact, she seemed more relaxed than he'd seen her since they met. He let loose a little sigh of relief. Even though she'd reassured him last night, a part of him had still expected to wake up and have her be distant or flinch from him or *something*.

But she hadn't.

"Come here." He pulled her into his lap, needing to touch her. It was more comfort than sexual, and that, too, was a gift. He stroked a hand down her spine and pressed a kiss to her temple. "You are amazing."

"I know." She laughed. "Oh, wait, sorry. I mean, thank you, Sir."

"Always something clever to say." He kissed the spot behind her ear. "Unless you're on my cock."

"Hey, now." She wiggled out of his arms, and he let her go, curious to see what she'd do. Sara turned and waved a finger at him. "None of that until I get my coffee."

"You put coffee before your Sir?" He rose slowly, enjoying himself far too much. She had a twinkle in her eye, and he couldn't stop grinning despite putting some growl into his voice. "Your priorities are skewed."

"I don't think so." She took another sip, watching him over the rim of her cup. "Coffee is so warm and delicious and makes me feel good."

"Sara."

"I mean, you have two out of three, so I guess that's sort of okay." She took a step back, and then another, and he shadowed the movement. "Though coffee doesn't stalk me with *that* look on its face."

"Coffee's loss. Come here."

She ducked out of his reach and set her mug on a nearby table. "I don't think so."

He rushed forward, but she was already gone, diving in the water. Z wasted no time shedding his pants and following her in. He'd spent too much time being half drowned by the ocean to completely love the water anymore, but this wasn't some mission to the depths of hell. This was…play, and fun, and laughter. He surfaced in time to get splashed in the face, Sara's giggles ringing through the room.

He dove again, swimming beneath the surface toward her. She was quick, but he was quicker. He snatched her ankle and dragged her down as he pushed up. This time, she was the one met with a splash when she surfaced. She went under, and he had half a second to wonder if he'd pushed too hard, but then he felt clever hands running up his thighs. He held as still as he could while treading water, but it was damned difficult with her stroking his cock like *that*. She squeezed, and he groaned and went under.

Fucking enough.

He hooked her around the waist and dragged her to shallower water. His feet barely touched the bottom and she was wrapped around him, kissing up his jaw to his mouth. "God, you make me so hot, Z…" Sara leaned back, a small frown on her face. "I just realized I don't know your full name."

"Zebadiah Loreto."

"Zebadiah," she breathed. "That's strangely hot."

The way she said his name was strangely hot, too. He kissed her, using his grip on her hips to line her up exactly where he wanted her. She was so warm compared to the water around them, and her pussy was warmer yet. He walked them up the incline to the wide steps leading out of the shallow end, and sat on the second one. It left everything above the tops of his thighs above the water, which was fucking perfect as far as he was concerned.

"Zebadiah." Fuck, she seemed to like saying his full name as much as he liked hearing it come off her lips. "Let me have my wicked way with you. Please?"

As if he could deny her anything right then. Z felt strange and out of control in a completely different way than he had been so far that week. "Do it."

She backed down until she was between his thighs. Without hesitation, she took his cock into her mouth. With the water lapping at his hips and her fingers digging into his thighs, the contrasting sensations only served to heighten the pleasure. He leaned back, bracing his arms on the concrete and letting her take the reins. She sucked him deeper, until his cock bumped the back of her throat, making him groan. "That's it, Sara. Take all of me."

She licked and sucked and drove him damn crazy, and he had to dig his fingers into the edge of the pool to keep from hauling her up his body and taking her right there. As soon as the thought crossed his mind, he wondered why the hell he was holding back. He wanted her.

He was going to take her.

Chapter Fifteen

Sara barely had time to get into the feeling of Z's cock in her mouth when he dragged her up his body to straddle him. He took her mouth in a slow, drugging kiss, his tongue playing along hers as if he had all the time in the world. As if he was never going to get enough. His hands urged her to slide up and down against his cock, its ridge lining up perfectly with her clit.

There was something so damn forbidden about this, about them miming sex without any barrier between them, that her entire body zinged with desire unlike any she'd ever known. Every inch of her skin was on fire, the feeling heightened by the drag of her nipples against his chest, the imprint of each of his fingers on her ass, his cock between her legs, his tongue in her mouth. She wanted. God Almighty, she wanted.

She slid against him faster, chasing the delicious feeling building inside her. "Why can't I get enough of you?"

"I don't know." He jerked her up a little higher than she'd been before, taking her nipple in his mouth.

"*Shit*." She went wild, holding him against her, her hips rolling, seeking… There. His cock notched in her entrance. A small voice inside her was screaming that this was a terrible idea, but she didn't care. Before she could think too hard on that, she slammed down, sheathing him deep inside her.

And, damn, it was even better than she could have imagined to having him filling her with nothing between them.

His hands spasmed. "Sara, we shouldn't." Despite his words, he didn't push her away or try to withdraw. Instead, he thrust ever so slightly, rocking against her.

"I know." But she couldn't stop. The fact they shouldn't be doing this only spurred her need for him higher. She kissed him, needing to be as close to Z as she possibly could. Her orgasm loomed, but she didn't want to stop riding this edge of pleasure so sharp it was almost pain.

She leaned back, keeping a grip on his shoulders, needing to see his face. As she rode his cock his gaze centered on the spot where their bodies joined. He cupped her breasts, lightly rolling her nipples between his fingers. "You are so fucking beautiful."

With him looking at her like that, she'd never *felt* more beautiful.

His slid his hands down between them, holding the spot where her thighs met her ass. Before she could adjust, he lifted her, keeping her splayed wide, until only the crown of his cock remained inside her. She looked down, mesmerized by the picture they made. Then Z started the slow slide down, spearing her inch by torturous inch. It was decadent and thrilling and she fought against his hold to take him all.

"Not yet, sweetheart. Soon." Before sheathing himself completely, he lifted her and started the process again.

Her breath sobbed from her throat. "Please. I need you." When he remained unrelenting, lifting her a third time, she dug her nails into his shoulders. "Zebadiah, *please*."

"Yes." He brought her down hard and shifted his grip to grind her against him, sending her flying into oblivion. She cried out, clinging to him as he milked every single shudder from her. And then he turned them, bracing her against the side of the pool as he pounded into her. She kissed his neck, still half dazed from her release. *We should stop.* But she didn't say the words. Refused to.

He cursed as he came, his fingers digging in to her hips even as she kept him close with her legs around his waist. He wrapped his arms around her, holding her so tightly she could barely breathe.

They stayed like that for a long time, long after their breathing had returned to normal, long after the water had cooled their bodies. She kept her eyes closed and her forehead against his shoulder, not wanting to look at him for fear of what she'd see on his face. What they'd just done was unbearably stupid, birth control or not. But she didn't want to dirty it with real life. Not yet.

He stroked a hand over her hair. "Talk to me."

"I'm on birth control." It was out before she could stop herself. "And I'm clean. I'm always careful, and I get tested on such a regular basis, it's downright paranoid."

"I'm clean, too." He held her tighter. "I haven't been with anyone in months—not since the most recent test."

Knowing that was a relief, but it didn't make what they'd done any less stupid. She *never* lost control like this, never put herself in a position where the end results were up for grabs. It left her cold that she'd barely questioned the intelligence of doing it this time, trusting Z or not. No, knowing that it was forbidden only made it hotter.

She was so fucked up.

He finally pulled out and let her off the pool wall. "Let's get something to eat."

He led her out of the pool and patted her dry, all the while her mind was still whirling. It was tempting to go hide in her room until she felt better about things—too tempting. Z wouldn't stand for it, though. And, more than that, she knew that she'd just work herself up into a panic if she had too much time to think. It was over and done with, and she should be thanking God that she wouldn't be seeing any permanent consequences for it. That said... She stopped him with her hand on his arm. "Z?"

"Yeah?"

"Can we... I mean..." She took a deep breath. "I don't want to stop using condoms."

Immediately, he wrapped his arms around her. "We won't. That was a one-time thing, okay? I'm not going to say it wasn't some of the hottest sex in my life, but we won't go bareback until you're comfortable with it."

She let it slide that he assumed she'd *ever* be comfortable with it. That was a talk for another day. Right now, she just had to ride out her sudden anxiety until it dissipated. "Do you cook?"

"Only if MREs and cold cereal counts. And I know how you feel about cold cereal." He kept his arm around her as they walked back into the house to the kitchen.

She laughed, glad that he was keeping things light. She'd

never met a man who could read her like Z could. "I don't think we have MREs hidden away anywhere around here—though I wouldn't be surprised, knowing Uncle Rodger. Either way, I vote for something a little more substantial. Think you can swing PB and J?"

"Consider it done." He guided her to the stool he'd occupied yesterday while she was making breakfast. The silence stretched out as he put together two sandwiches. He passed over one of them. "Do you want to talk about it?"

She took her time chewing and swallowed. "No."

"Okay. If you change your mind, let me know."

"Will do." She had no intention of getting into *that* conversation if she could help it. She already felt spooked and twisted up. Adding a potential talk about the future on top of it? No, thanks.

She'd take things one day at a time. It was the only way she knew how to move forward with Z without losing her damn mind.

...

After breakfast, Z wasn't sure where to go from there. He wanted to talk about what they'd done in the pool. Fuck, he couldn't believe he'd been stupid enough to lose control and fuck Sara without a condom. From the stilted conversation afterward, he gathered that there was no risk of pregnancy, but it was still unforgivable. He'd put her in jeopardy, even if it was unintentional.

But that was obviously the last thing *she* wanted to talk about. It was in every tense line of her body when he asked her about it, and the way she wouldn't meet his gaze. It stung a little, but he'd respect her wishes.

For now.

"Since the power's back on, do you want to watch a movie?"

She braved a smile. "Sure."

On the first day, he'd found a theater room in the west wing of the house. Its tiered floor had wide chaise lounge chairs that could easily fit two people. While Sara looked through the extensive movie collection, he found a thick knitted blanket and tossed it onto the couch in the middle.

"Thoughts on *Aliens*?"

"The best of the *Alien* movies."

This time, her grin was much more real. "I knew I liked you. *Aliens*, it is." She popped it into the system, which looked like something out of a science fiction movie, and came to sit next to him. He tucked her against his side and pulled the blanket over both of them. A few minutes later, they were watching Ellen Ripley being recovered from deep space.

He'd always liked this movie, but he liked it with Sara a thousand times more. She didn't feel the need to keep up an ongoing commentary, and despite the fact that she'd seen it enough to occasionally mutter lines under her breath, she still jumped at some of the parts. Not to mention she eased closer to him throughout the first half, until she was nearly in his lap.

Fuck, he could get used to this.

If he had a woman like Sara, he might actually look forward to coming home after every mission, instead of dreading it. And she was independent enough to live her own life while he was gone, without feeling like he was abandoning her. It was very feasible that they could make this work—really work.

His phone started ringing, and for the first time in seven years, he was tempted to let it go to voicemail. He couldn't, though. There were people depending on him, and ignoring their calls wasn't the mark of a good leader. With a sigh, he answered. "Loreto."

"We got a problem."

Shit. He'd left Andrew in charge while he was handling bodyguard duty for Sara, and he wouldn't be calling him for anything less than a sky-is-falling emergency. "Hold on." He kissed Sara and climbed off the couch. As soon as the theater door shut behind him, he said, "Tell me."

"Team you sent to retrieve the package hasn't reported in."

Fuck. He scrubbed a hand over his face. "They should have reported in damn near twelve hours ago. What took you so long to call me?"

"I was still tracking their movement via satellite, but they went dark thirty minutes ago."

He closed his eyes. "Okay. Call in Garrett and Rick. I'll be there in…" He checked his watch. "Four hours. Update me when you have news."

"Will do."

He hung up, hating that this shit had come along when things were finally calming down with Sara. But his men might be in trouble, and he sure as fuck wasn't going to leave them hanging out to dry. He called Joe. "There's trouble. I need you at the house in fifteen."

"Want me to come in hot?"

"No. The trouble isn't here." He pocketed his phone and went back into the media room. "Sara, we need to talk."

She shut off the movie and turned to face him. "What's going on?"

"You're safe." He needed her to know that, if nothing else. "But some of my men aren't."

"You have to go." There was no condemnation in her voice, no guilt-tripping. Just calm acceptance.

"Joe's coming in from the road to stay with you until I can get back."

"Then I need some clothes."

He followed her upstairs to her room and watched her pull on a pair of sweats and a t-shirt. "I'll be back as soon as I can."

"I know." She went up on her tiptoes to kiss him. "Go, Z. I'm safe enough here, and it sounds like they need you a whole hell of a lot."

"They might." But he still didn't leave the room. Not yet. "Sara." He waited for her to look at him. "As soon as I get back, we're going to have a conversation."

She went still. "I figured."

"I mean to keep you, sweetheart. And don't you forget it." He kissed her one last time and walked out of the room before she had a chance to reply.

Chapter Sixteen

The next week passed at a snail's pace. Sara avoided Z's man, Joe, as much as she could. He was nice enough, but all he did was remind her that the man she really wanted to be spending time with was off in some unknown part of the world, putting himself in danger. And there wasn't a damn thing she could do about it, because she was stuck here.

Not that she could do much about it even if she was back in the city. Her skill set leaned toward cleaning up messes made by other people—not saving soldiers.

"I thought I'd find you stewing."

She looked up as Ridley walked into the theater room. "What are you doing here?"

"Stewing. Garrett went with Z." She walked down the aisle and plopped next to Sara. "When he's gone on retrieval missions like this, he can't risk calling to update me, so I'm driving myself out of my mind."

"Sounds familiar." Even her favorite comfort movies—

Resident Evil: Apocalypse, Tucker & Dale vs. Evil, and *A Perfect Getaway*—weren't enough to actually *comfort* her. She kept wondering where in the world Z was, and if he was okay, and if she should be freaking out. The only upside was that she was so busy worrying about him, she hadn't had a chance to worry about herself. "How do you handle this happening over and over again?"

"I don't know. It goes with the territory of being with Garrett, so I power through." Ridley sighed. "And he has the tendency to send people over to check on me and to keep me distracted."

Sara had been swimming more laps in the last week than she had in the last three months combined. She'd been grateful time and time again that there had been a swimsuit in the bag her friend packed for her—teasing Z was all well and good, but the thought of Joe seeing her skinny dipping made her skin crawl. There was nothing wrong with him, exactly, other than the fact he was too *not* Z. She flopped back against the pillow. "I think I went and fell for him."

"I *knew* it. I knew there was something going on—well, something more than sex. That's kind of a given with you."

"Hey!" She grinned. "Only mostly. But he's something else. He makes me crazy and uncomfortable and so hot, I can't see straight."

"I'm familiar with the feeling."

"Since you're talking about my brother, I'm just going to pretend I didn't hear that." She traced the stitched pattern on the couch. "What am I going to do? I'm not cut out for relationships." Then again, neither was he. They were both people who'd been broken and crawled back from the verge. Maybe they were just broken enough to fit each other.

"You figure it out as you go."

That didn't sound so bad. She could take one day at a time. No crazy leaps forward into uncertainty. There was enough of that shit in the future without making it harder on themselves. "Maybe I'll do just that."

"That's my girl." Ridley settled in next to her. "What are we watching?"

"*Mean Girls*."

"It's like you knew I was coming."

They spent the rest of the day chatting and snacking and watching cheesy movies and, by the time her friend called it a night and bunkered down in one of the other rooms, Sara felt worlds better. She could do this. It might not be amazing and wonderful all the time, but she could definitely give things with Z an honest try.

She was almost asleep when her phone rang. "Hello?"

"Sara."

Her heart leaped into her throat. "Z? Are you back?"

"No." He sighed, the line crackling. "The situation is more complicated than I'd thought it would be. I'm out for another week, possibly more. But I wanted to hear your voice."

Yeah, that giddy feeling in her stomach was definitely her falling head over heels for the man. She settled on her side. "I'm glad you called."

"I can't talk long but… I'm thinking of you. All the fucking time."

"Me, too." Her breath hitched, but she forced it out in a smooth exhale. Keeping things locked down and putting on a strong face was important, even if the thought of not seeing him for another week—or longer—was a horrible one. "Stay safe, okay? I'm counting on that date you promised me."

"I wouldn't miss it for the world." She heard something that sounded suspiciously like gunfire in the background. He cursed. "I've got to go. Touch yourself when you think about me tonight." Then he was gone, the phone dead against her ear.

She wasn't sure if she should laugh or cry. He was obviously in danger, but just as obviously, he wanted to make *her* feel better. She rolled onto her back. "Well, hell. I think that was an order." And she wanted to be able to tell him she came while thinking about him next time they talked.

She'd just slid off her sweats when her phone rang again. *What now?* She glanced at the display and frowned. "Uncle Rodger?"

"I know it's late, but I thought you'd want this news as soon as possible. Mr. Nord has called off his goons—with the condition that you stay the hell away from him. Can you do that?"

It stuck in her throat that the man was getting away with cheating and lying, but he'd proven himself more than a match for her, and she wouldn't be able to come home unless she agreed. So that's exactly what she did. "Okay."

"Good. Take tomorrow, but I expect you in the office the day after."

Getting back to work would be the perfect distraction to keep her from thinking too hard about where Z was. "Sounds good."

"Night, Sara." He hung up.

She lay back with a smile. Z was safe for now, and thinking of her, and her exile was officially over. God, it was going to be good to go home.

...

Z had been back in the US for barely twenty-four hours when he got off the train in New York. He'd stopped home to shower, sleep a few hours, and change, but he hadn't wanted to wait to see Sara. Four fucking weeks since he'd seen her last. Their stolen conversations had helped, but they were a temporary patch for a problem that only having her in his arms could fix. His men were safe, and the mission was a success, but it had taken too long. He'd never felt that way before.

But, then, he'd never had someone waiting for him to come home.

He knocked on her door, hoping like hell she was actually home. He'd wanted to surprise her, so he hadn't called first. Sure enough, it burst open and Sara was in his arms half a second later. He held her close, letting it finally sink in. She was *his*. And he was here, and they were both safe for the first time since they'd met.

Z stepped into the apartment and kicked the door shut behind him. She was already working on his pants. "I need you inside me."

"Yes." He had the presence of mind to lock the damn door, but then she was tugging him past the couch to her bedroom. It was all new furniture, the old ruined during the break in.

"Hurry up." She yanked off her dress, quickly followed by her panties and bra. He got his shirt off and then she was kissing him again. "God, Zebadiah, I missed the hell out of you."

The combination of his given name and the rest of what she said had him holding her tightly against him. "I missed you, too." Two seconds later he was naked and they were on her bed.

She scrambled for the nightstand, and came up with a condom. "Next time we'll go slow."

"Who's in charge here?"

"Right now? Me." She rolled the condom on and had him inside her before he could think of a good reason to argue. It turned out there wasn't one, not when she was warm and tight around him. She shifted, taking him deeper yet. "God, I missed this nearly as much as I missed you."

He pulled her down for a kiss, and rolled them. Even now, he could barely believe he was here, inside her, with her whispering such sweet shit in his ear. He pulled almost all the way out, and then thrust into her. As her eyes started to slide shut, he framed her face with his hands. "Eyes open, sweetheart. I missed those baby blues."

"You missed a lot."

"Damn straight." He kept going, conscious of her rising to meet each stroke, their bodies completely attuned to each other despite the separation. He drew it out as long as he possibly could, enjoying their closeness, their intimacy, but he knew the second she approached the point of no return. "Come for me, Sara. I've been dying to feel your tight pussy clenching around my cock. I've been dreaming about it for four fucking weeks."

She kissed him as her body went wild, her pussy doing exactly as he'd described, milking him until he couldn't control his thrusts, until he gave in with a curse, coming so hard it felt like the top of his head was going to explode.

When he could move again, he rolled onto his side, taking her with him. "Damn."

"Mmm." She kissed his throat. "Why didn't you call me to tell me you were back?"

"I wanted to surprise you."

She laughed. "That was one hell of a surprise." With a sigh, she stretched. "I hope you're hungry. I was just going to run out and get something to eat."

It was on the tip of his tongue to tell her to stay and answer the need already hardening his cock again, but there was more than one kind of need. "How about takeout?"

She seemed to consider. "Normally, I'd say yes, but I'm jonesing for some taco truck. I've been thinking about it all day."

"Far be it for me to keep you from this taco truck of course." He sat up. "Shower first."

"But…"

"You had your chance to be in charge, sweetheart." He grabbed another condom and followed her into the bathroom. For all her protests, she wasted no time getting the water running and pulling him in behind her.

"Did I mention how much I missed you? Because I'm holding off on really excellent tacos for you."

"Your sacrifice is appreciated." He pushed her until her back rested against the tile and went to his knees in front of her, maneuvering one of her legs up to drape over his shoulder, and baring her to his mouth.

She cried out as he tasted her. "Is every homecoming going to be like this?"

Homecoming. Fuck, he liked the sound of that. He sucked her clit into his mouth, rolling the sensitive bundle of nerves between his lips. "Yes."

"Good." She wobbled, but he kept her up with one hand

on her thigh and the other on her hip. Using his hold to open her wider, he fucked her with his tongue the same way he had with his cock, slow and deep. She unraveled around him, her hands sliding over the back of his head to keep him in contact as she shuddered. Like he was going anywhere.

He drew her orgasm out until the only thing keeping her off the floor was his strength. Then he pushed to his feet, paused to roll on the condom, and buried himself deep inside her. He'd never get tired of this. *Never.* Z would move mountains and commit terrible acts to keep Sara in his life. He wouldn't even hesitate.

He took her in the shower until they were both barely standing, until they were clinging to each other and beyond words. Z smiled against her hair. This, right in that moment, was perfection.

Chapter Seventeen

Sara took another bite of quesadilla and sighed in bliss. "This day couldn't get any better."

"I'd find that more flattering if I didn't think you were talking about the food." Z leaned back against the bench they'd taken after getting their order.

She pretended to consider. "You were pretty good, too."

He laughed. "Nice to know."

It was like the last four weeks of separation had never happened. She'd wondered if things would be different or awkward when he came back, but it was just as comfortable as it'd been while they were locked away in the house. Maybe this really *would* work.

She took another bite, closing her eyes and fighting down a moan. God, when had taco truck tacos ever tasted this good? She didn't even *like* food served out of a truck normally, but it had been hitting the spot in a major way the last few days.

"Sara."

She opened her eyes, and frowned at the look on his face. Apparently he hadn't forgotten his promise-slash-threat that they were going to have a talk when he got back. Part of her wanted to hold it off as long as possible, but it was coming whether she liked it not. "Yeah?"

"I want you. Not just stolen moments in exile, as you called it. I want the homecomings and dinners and all of it."

Longing wrapped around her chest and squeezed. She took a sip of her soda "I thought we were taking it one day at a time." *That* she could handle. But he sounded like he wanted…everything. Jumping from a stolen week to *everything* was just that—a massive jump. The first flutters of panic started in her stomach.

For a second, it looked like he'd argue, but Z finally sighed. "You're right. We are."

Thank God. "Okay. Good." She took another bite, pretending things hadn't taken a turn for the horribly awkward. But then there was nothing else to eat, and she was stuffed, so she couldn't exactly order something else to hold off dealing with whatever the strange look on Z's face meant. Might as well get it over with. "What are you thinking?"

"I was remembering our time in the pool."

Her body heated as she was transported back to the feeling of him inside her, the chilly water a direct counterpoint to the heat that he roused better than any man she'd ever known. Just thinking about it was enough to have her shifting in her seat, and calculating how long it would take them to get back to her apartment. "That was pretty great."

"It was." He zeroed in on her face. "I have to ask, though… You've had your period?"

The feel-good fantasy disappeared in a puff of smoke. She glared. "What the hell kind of question is that? I told you I was on birth control."

"I'm not doubting you."

"Good. Because it's like ninety nine percent—" Her words dried up, a strange buzzing starting in her ears. It had been a hell of a month. She'd come back to the city and hit the ground running, barely taking time to sleep and eat in between Uncle Rodger running her ragged. And she'd loved it, because it helped keep the ache of Z's absence at bay. Sara cleared her suddenly dry throat. She'd never been one of those women who felt compelled to track her periods, but even she could do basic math. The last one she'd had was weeks before her exile—the only reason she remembered that was because she'd been furious it ruined her plans to go out with a gorgeous bartender she'd had her eye on.

Which meant she hadn't had a period in well over seven weeks. "Oh God, this can't be happening."

If she'd thought Z had been focused before, it was nothing to how he looked at her now. "Tell me."

She didn't want to say it aloud. It was a silly, childish superstition—don't talk about the bad thing, and maybe it will go away—but she couldn't shake it. "It's not possible."

"*Sara.*"

"Look, women are late all the time. It doesn't mean anything."

The slow-dawning horror on his face didn't make her feel the slightest bit better, despite the fact that it was an exact match for the unfolding feelings in her chest. "You're pregnant."

"*Shut up.* I am not." The night air seemed determined to

close in on her, so she slid off the bench and damn near ran for the street. *I'm not pregnant. I* can't *be pregnant. Please, God, don't let me be pregnant.*

He caught up with her on the sidewalk and grabbed her arm, swinging her around to face him. "Talk to me."

"I'm not pre—" She couldn't even say the word, but she babbled on, reaching for something—anything—to prove this was all a bad dream. "I can't be. I'm not sick. The last time I threw up was New Year's Eve three years ago. I'm not napping or tired or *pregnant.*" She would have known if she was. Something would be drastically different if she was growing a life in her stomach. She pressed a hand there, finding it as flat as ever.

"There's only one way to find out."

"What?" He kept his grip on her arm, towing her down the street. She figured out his destination—the corner store—and dug in her heels. "No. Z, please, don't."

"If you are carrying my child, I damn well want to know." Each word was clipped and fierce.

"Maybe it's not yours." He turned a fierce glare on her, and she wilted on the spot. "Okay, fine, *if* I were, then it's *probably* yours." In reality, it was definitely his. She'd never had unprotected sex before, never let herself get so carried away that she cared more about getting a man inside her than getting on a condom. Plus, she might not be awesome at math, but she could put two and two together. It had to be his.

"Stop talking." With that, he dragged her through the door and down the aisle to the pregnancy tests.

• • •

Once they got back to her apartment, Z couldn't sit still while he waited for Sara to get out of the bathroom. He'd damn near followed her in, but she'd flatly told him that she'd pee in front of him over her dead body. He made another turn and glared at the closed door. She'd been in there an awfully long time.

And she might be having his baby.

He could barely wrap his mind around it. Children had been something he wanted—*before*. Before Jennifer ripped out his heart. Before his life fell apart. Before he lost everything and hit rock bottom. After he'd crawled back to what passed for a normal life, he hadn't put much thought into that tired old dream. Until Sara, he hadn't ever planned on letting a woman close enough to date, let alone have kids with.

This was sure as fuck a long way off from taking one day at a time.

He'd wanted a life with this woman, yes. But on *his* terms. It was a naive thought, maybe, but it had still been what he'd planned when he took the train up here—to convince her to give them a real shot. Z shook his head. A baby. A motherfucking *baby*. He didn't know the first thing about kids. What the hell was he going to do with one of his own?

The door opened, and he spun to face her. One look at her expression was all it took to get his answer. "You're pregnant."

"I'm pregnant." She wrapped her arms around herself and crossed to sit on the couch. "This can't be happening."

"You can say that all you want to, but the fact remains that it *is* happening." He started to sit next to her but she held up her hand. Trying not to be pissed, he sat on the chair across from her. "We need to talk about this."

"I need a minute."

"Sara—"

"No." Her voice took on a shrill tone he'd never heard before, even when that CEO wanted to drive her out of town. "You can damn well give me a minute to catch my breath after learning that my fucking life is ruined."

Ruined.

He'd be the first to admit that this had never been part of the plan, and wasn't the most ideal of outcomes, but *ruined*? "It's a baby, not a death sentence."

"You *would* say that." She pulled her knees to her chest. "You're a man who barely stays in one place long enough to call it home. This isn't going to change a damn thing in your life."

"That's not fair." This was going to change a whole hell of a lot.

"It's the truth. I'm the one who has to carry this baby."

"You mean—"

"I'm keeping it. Unless you have a problem with that?" The look she shot him was pure venom. Coming from a woman who had smiled so sweetly and with whom he'd shared so much in such a short time… Yeah, it pissed him off.

He pushed to his feet, trying to keep a hold of his temper. "Don't make me the villain. It took both of us to get to this point."

"Maybe it did, but I'm the only one who's actually chained down by the consequences." She slapped a hand over her mouth. "Okay, that wasn't fair."

But it was too late. His anger slipped its leash. "I didn't hear you telling me to stop when you slid my cock home."

He wanted to throw something, to punch something, but kept the impulse tightly leashed. "No, you were begging me for more while your pussy milked me for everything I had."

"So this is *my* fault?" Now she was on her feet. "That's rich. And cliché. You wanted it badly enough when we were in the middle of it, but now that there are actual consequences, you're playing the blame game."

"No, I'm fucking not, Sara. And I'm not leaving you to shoulder this alone." He clenched and unclenched his fists. "We have to get married."

Her eyes went wide. "Are you insane?"

"I'm not going to have my kid born a bastard."

"Holy fucking shit, you're serious." She threw up her hands. "Zebadiah, let me clue you in on a little something. We're in the twenty-first century. Women get pregnant, give birth, and raise kids without fathers around all the time — and they don't even bother to tattoo a scarlet "A" on their chest while they do it."

"Marry me."

"No way. We don't even know each other. Sure, we can fuck like porn stars, but that doesn't make a lasting relationship."

"Don't dirty this. I want you. I've wanted you since the moment I laid eyes on you. Marry me." He moved closer, but she skirted the edge of the coffee table.

As if she was afraid of him.

That stopped him cold. "Sara—"

"Stop. Just stop." She held up a hand. "You're throwing everything but the kitchen sink at me, and it's too much. I need time to think."

What she meant was she needed time to talk to her other people to see how she fucking felt. Z shook his head. No, that wasn't Sara. That was Jennifer. But the two nightmares were merging into one, and he had the horrible feeling that if he didn't get an answer right this goddamn second, she was going to be lost to him forever. "This is the last time I'm going to ask you—marry me."

"*No*."

The rejection cut him to the soul. "So I'm good enough to fuck, but not to be in a relationship with?"

She held herself so tightly, it was as if she thought she'd fly apart at the slightest provocation. "There's a hell of a difference between a relationship and a marriage, Z. You're making it sound like it's all or nothing. I can't do things that way."

"There's a baby involved. It *is* all or nothing." If she didn't marry him, there was a chance she could cut him out of the entire process. He didn't *think* Sara would pull a stunt like that, but it wasn't a risk he was willing to take.

Her mouth tightened. "Get out. I'm not having this conversation with you right now."

"I walk out, this is over." Common sense had no place here. All he could think was that she was rejecting him—pushing him out the door while the dream he hadn't realized he still held onto shattered around him. She wouldn't marry him.

"If one fight is all it takes to drive you off, then go. Better now than later."

He wanted to shake her, to kiss her, to fuck her until she saw reason, but none of those were options, not when she was edging away from him like that. *Fuck*. "You want me gone, I'm gone."

"Just like that." She laughed hoarsely. "I should have

known." Sara lifted the necklace he'd given her from her neck and threw it at him. "Then leave, if that's what you want."

It wasn't what he wanted. Fuck, couldn't she see that? But staying here meant continuing to fight, and he could actually see her getting farther and farther from him. He scooped up the necklace and stalked out the door.

Chapter Eighteen

Sara looked around the clinic waiting room, decorated in cheery yellow colors, and wanted to turn around and leave. Two weeks since she saw Z last, and she still had a hard time wrapping her mind around the fact that this was really happening. It had seemed like some horrible waking nightmare, but six pee tests later, and there was no denying the fact that she was really pregnant.

She turned to Ridley. "Thanks for coming with me."

"As if there was any doubt." She bit her lip. "Though you know Z would have come if you asked."

"He's not speaking to me." There had been exactly one call in fourteen days, and it started out with him proposing again and went downhill from there. He didn't get it. Marriage wasn't the answer. Maybe if her parents had held off a little longer before they got married and had kids, they would have realized they weren't a good match. Except that logic didn't fit, because they'd been *fine* for twenty years. She and Z couldn't even be fine for two months—how the hell were they supposed to make a relationship that lasted their entire lives?

The short answer was that they couldn't.

And she would rather her parents had never gotten married than to find out her mother lived a lie of happiness for twenty freaking years before she couldn't take it anymore. Better to save their unborn baby the horrible trauma of realizing the parents he or she loved so much didn't actually love each other. She smiled bitterly. It'd save the kid a fortune in therapy bills.

"Sara—"

"I don't really want to talk about it."

"Well, tough shit."

She turned to look at her friend. "Is this where you tell me that he's misunderstood and that we could totally make a life together?"

Ridley rolled her eyes. "Don't be stupid. He was an idiot for proposing. You don't get married for a baby—it's not a lasting reason to walk down the aisle."

It shouldn't make her so pathetically grateful that *someone* agreed with her, but it did. "Then what's the problem?"

"Oh, I don't know, how about the fact that everyone's ready to light some torches, grab some pitchforks, and hunt Z to the end of the earth? You have *no* idea what kind of moves I've had to pull to keep Garrett from doing something we'd all regret. And that's not even getting into Will."

She'd been avoiding her brothers even more thoroughly than she'd been avoiding Z. Sara already knew what they'd say—she was irresponsible and stupid and had finally gotten herself into a mess that no one could fix. She could deal with that, though. What she *wouldn't be able to* forgive was if one of them went so far as to suggest she get an abortion to take care of the issue—or that she was an even bigger idiot for refusing to consider it.

She pressed her hand to her stomach. As irrational as it was—and as much as this baby had already complicated the hell out of her life—she couldn't make that choice. "It's none of their business."

"Tell that to *them*. Oh wait, you can't, because you're too busy hiding in your apartment and feeling sorry for yourself."

She glared. "You don't know what I'm going through."

"Oh, please. Spare me. I know *you*. Was this unplanned? Sure. Are you going to make the best of it and come out on top? No doubt about it."

"That's a seriously backhanded compliment." Because Ridley was right. She *had* been bunkered down, feeling sorry for herself. Every time she thought about Z, a hole opened in her chest that felt like it'd consume her if she made one wrong move. She slouched in her seat and wrapped her arms around herself. "He wouldn't even talk to me about it. He just laid out terms—marry him or he's gone."

"Z's a man who likes a plan." Her friend shrugged. "He was freaking the hell out."

"We talked last week and it was more of the same—marry me or else. I can't do that. I refuse to." But the thought of spending the rest of her life with him on the fringes hurt, too. A lot more than she ever could have anticipated. "I don't see why we can't just go slow. I liked spending time with him. I thought it might really be *something*, you know? Something to break all my rules for."

"Did you say that to him? Or did you just dig in your heels and start yelling for him to get out?"

Sara shot her a look. "He doesn't want to talk."

"Maybe he's just being man-stupid and doesn't know how. He's as freaked out as you are. Give him a break."

Easier said than done. His words rattled around in her head, creating a tempest that kept provoking her to respond first and think last. She *knew* what was causing his hair trigger, but that didn't magically erase some of the stupid stuff he'd thrown at her. She was about to tell Ridley just that, but a nurse poked her head into the waiting room. "Sara Reaver?"

"Yes?"

"Follow me."

They ended up in a room identical to every other exam room she'd ever been to. As they waited, it struck her that Z *should* be here. This was his baby as much as it was hers—a thought she kept avoiding. It was so easy to think of it as she and baby against the world, but that wasn't the truth. If she let him, Z would be in her corner. Hell, he'd stand against anything the world decided to throw at them and probably crush it beneath his boot. The thought made her smile.

The door opened and the doctor came in. He was the same one she'd been seeing since she hit puberty, and it seemed like he'd stopped aging somewhere around sixty, because she had no idea how old he was now. He smiled at her, his eyes happy. "Congratulations, Sara. Would you like to see your baby?"

...

Z woke to find two blond men towering over him. Normally, he'd be up and moving before they had a chance to realize he was no longer sleeping, but this conversation was several weeks overdue. "Garrett. Will."

"What the fuck is wrong with you?" Garrett grabbed his shirt and hauled him to his feet. "Our goddamn baby sister, Z. Of all the women in the world, *she's* the one you couldn't keep your dick in your pants around?" He pulled back his right hand, but his twin stopped him before he made contact.

"Garrett, enough." Will detached his hand and shoved Z back onto the couch. "How are you going to make this right?"

Make this right? Hadn't that been exactly what he'd been trying to do from the moment he found out Sara was pregnant? But she blocked every attempt he made, and had an argument ready every time he so much as brought up marriage. She wasn't going to let him put a ring on her finger. She'd made *that* abundantly clear. Garrett took a step forward like he was going to try to clobber Z again, and Z made no move to block it. He deserved to be clobbered.

"*Enough.*"

Garrett spun on his twin. "No, it's not enough. I don't get how you can be so fucking calm about this shit. Sara is having a goddamn baby and it's *his*."

No expression showed on Will's face. Z had never met a colder son of a bitch than Garrett's twin. "Because it's Sara. She's more than capable of taking care of herself and making her own decisions."

"He took advantage—"

"Christ, will you listen to yourself? If anyone was taken advantage of, it was Z."

Z, who was still standing in the room, wondered if the

world had gone mad around him. He'd fully expected Garrett to show up—possibly with his twin in tow—and beat the living shit out of him. Hell, he'd relished the idea. At least then he'd have some physical pain to distract him from the soul ache that seemed to grow every day.

Garrett cursed. "None of this changes the fact that Sara is pregnant and dealing with this shit alone while he sits here and mopes." He pointed a finger at Z.

It was as if the thing that had been building in him for the last two weeks broke. "She won't fucking let me! You think I haven't tried? I've yelled, pleaded, and tried to reason with her. She won't listen and won't compromise." And every time she said no, it was like she'd stabbed him in the chest.

Will crossed his arms over his chest. "And what compromises have you offered?"

Z opened his mouth to tell him, but stopped. What *had* he offered? Marriage. Over and over again, until he thought his head might explode. "She won't marry me."

"No shit." Garrett scrubbed a hand over his face. "I bet you just beat away at that point and never stopped to consider other options." He caught both men staring. "What? If I had my way, our baby sister would be in a convent right now and never would have met you. Or, hell, she'd say yes to marrying your dumb ass. You might be a dick, but you're loyal to a fault. I know that, even if I'm so pissed, I can't see straight."

He wouldn't be saying that if he knew the truth. Even knowing he should keep his damn mouth shut, Z said, "I don't deserve her."

"No one does." Garrett glared. "But I sure as hell hope

you aren't about to trot out that shit that happened with your ex to prove it. Yeah, I know about that. Don't look so fucking surprised. I've known about it for years."

"But—"

Will cut in. "Marriage is not currently an option, no matter what you or my twin want. So come up with another solution, Z, and quickly. If you don't, you're liable to miss out on something irreplaceable." He grabbed Garrett's shoulder and dragged him out of the house, leaving Z staring after them.

Didn't they realize he *knew* Sara was slipping through his fingers? He wasn't sleeping, was barely eating, was unable to think about anything beyond that. Even before the pregnancy, he knew he'd wanted her in his life. The presence of a baby hadn't changed that—it had just sped up the process.

His phone chimed and he picked it up, finding a text from Garrett. *Figure your shit out. Fast.* It was paired with a forwarded picture. He stared at the ultrasound photo. It didn't look like much—a cluster of grays and white and black—but it was his baby. *His baby.* And he'd missed seeing this in person.

How much more was he willing to miss?

He shot to his feet. Nothing. The answer was nothing else. He had to figure out how to make this right with Sara. It was tempting as fuck to call her, but he had the feeling they'd just have a repeat of the same old fight. No, he had to bring something new to the mix to show her he actually listened to what she was saying. Something he had refused to do until now. He touched the necklace she'd thrown back at him before he left her apartment.

The twins were right. He'd fucked up. But now he knew how to fix it.

He grabbed his keys and headed for the door. It was time to make things right with Sara. If that meant compromising? Well, he could do that, because he had the long game in mind. Someday he *would* put a ring on Sara Reaver's finger. But, for now, he needed to focus on convincing her to carve out a spot in her life for him.

Chapter Nineteen

Sara propped her feet on her coffee table and dug her spoon into the ice cream she'd bought on the way home from the doctor. Everyone knew that pregnant women had some weird-ass cravings, but so far hers had been pretty mundane. She glanced at the ultrasound pictures that the tech had printed out for her. Tomorrow, she'd take a few pictures of them and send them to Z. She'd almost done it tonight, but she was exhausted and weirdly sore and didn't have it in her for another go round of him demanding that she marry him despite all her arguments that it was a terrible idea.

Her throat burned, and she took a bite of ice cream to stave off another crying jag. The crazy mood swings hadn't shown up until recently, but she already felt like she was PMSing on steroids. And the worst part was that all she wanted was Z, even though he was partially the cause.

It seemed like every time she closed her eyes, she was assaulted with how good it'd been to have his arms wrapped around her. He'd made her feel like she was the most important thing in the word and, more than that, *safe*. Sara couldn't remember the last time she'd felt truly safe. Oh, she wasn't ever in danger—the thing with Nord notwithstanding—but that peace only seemed to be within reach when she was with him.

Frankly, it made her resent the hell out of him.

Because he should be *here*, eating ice cream and watching *The Big Bang Theory* reruns and talking about their day. With her. And it was becoming increasingly clear that it was as much her fault as his that he wasn't. If neither one of them gave an inch, this would never work. The problem was, he kept demanding all or nothing, and she refused to marry him.

So where did that leave them?

A knock on the door startled her into dropping her spoon. "Shit." She picked it up and stood. Who was at her door at this hour? A flash of fear hit her in the stomach. Surely it wasn't someone from Nord? That threat was supposed to have passed, and she hadn't heard otherwise in the six weeks she'd been back.

But that didn't mean it was true.

She'd never been this paranoid before she'd acquired her little blueberry, but she couldn't shake the feeling that she should be diving for the fire escape instead of creeping up to peer out the peephole. When she recognized the dark face and pale green eyes staring back at her, she nearly yanked open the door and threw herself into his arms. Only the memory of how things had ended last time she did exactly that was enough to help her keep control.

She opened the door slowly, half expecting him to bully

his way inside, but he didn't move. "May I come in?"

There was something different about him—hesitant, almost, like he wasn't sure of his welcome. The burning in her throat got worse. "Sure."

He lifted a bag that she hadn't noticed until just then. "Ridley said you're still craving tacos from that truck."

At the mention of food, her mouth watered. "She's playing dirty."

"I'm not complaining." His smile was tight and far too brief. "Can we talk?"

Here they went again. She braced herself, but the disappointment lay heavy enough on her shoulders that even the delicious smells coming from the takeout couldn't dissipate it. "If you want."

"Sara." He waited for her to look at him. "I'm going to marry you." Her throat closed, but he kept going. "Someday. When you're ready."

She blinked. "What?"

"I pushed too hard with it, and I was wrong. It was a knee jerk reaction, though I know that doesn't excuse my pigheadedness. I'm sorry." He carefully set out the food, lining the cartons up in a row. "But I'm telling you right now, I'm in this for the long run. I know you might need time, but I'm not leaving you."

"Oh." Damn it, she could do better than that. She cleared her throat. "You seem to have it all figured out."

"I don't. I've made mistakes with you." He reached across the coffee table and took her hand. "Have I mentioned how sorry I am that I botched the whole conversation surrounding finding out you're pregnant?"

"You weren't the only one who made mistakes." It would

have been convenient if she could play the injured party and pretend she wasn't just as much in the wrong as he was, but it would be a lie. "I was losing my shit that day—and pretty much every day since. I said some horrible things to you."

"I brought you something else." He reached into his pocket with his free hand and brought out a small box. For a second she almost panicked, but then she realized it was too big to be a ring. Z opened it and turned so she could see inside. It was a smaller, daintier, version of the necklace she could see peeking out of the collar of his shirt. The same one he'd put around her neck back at the house where they'd shared a stolen week. He caught her questioning glance. "You said you want to take things day by day, and I can respect that, but this is my promise to you—and to my son or daughter you're carrying. I will be here, constant as the compass points north, no matter what happens. I've fallen head over heels for you, and I was almost fool enough to let you slip through my fingers. I won't make that mistake again."

She leaned forward and let him slip the necklace over her head. It fell to rest directly over her heart. She pressed her hand to it, fighting back the stupid hormones that had her eyes burning. "Z, I think that might be the most romantic thing anyone has ever said to me."

"It's the truth." He took a deep breath. "I know you might need time to think about it, but I'm prepared to wait as long as it takes…"

She was already shaking her head. "Stay. Please. It's been miserable without you, and I don't want to waste another minute apart because of stupid shit." She took his hand and led him around the coffee table to sit on the couch next to her. "Do you want to see pictures of the baby?"

His grin damn near lit up the room. "There's nothing I'd like more." He bent down until his head was level with her stomach. "You probably can't hear me, little one, but I'm your daddy. I'm not perfect, but I already love you more than I thought possible." He pressed a gentle kiss through the fabric of her tank top, and then rose to press an equally gentle kiss to her lips. "I'm going to enjoy the hell out of raising a family with you, Sara Reaver."

Epilogue

"Now, baby girl, we've gone over this." Z considered his daughter, who was happily gumming away on her fist with a very distinctive look on her face. "You're supposed to leave nasty surprises for your mother only."

"Good luck with that," Sara's voice floated from the kitchen.

"A man can dream." He lifted Ivy and gave her lower regions a cautious sniff. The scent that assaulted his nose was enough to have his eyes watering. "I thought baby shit wasn't supposed to stink while you were still breastfeeding." He'd read the damn books—every book he could get his hands on—and though they'd contradicted themselves more often than not, this was one thing they'd agreed on.

It was just his luck that they were apparently wrong.

"Just keep believing that while you're changing her diaper." Sara's amusement made him grin in spite of himself. Three months of shared sleepless nights had cemented their bond into something damn near unbreakable. She hadn't agreed to marry him yet, but he'd moved in right before Ivy was born, and their life was pretty fucking amazing as far as he was concerned.

He mock frowned at Ivy, but the expression turned to a stupid grin when her blue eyes—so like her mama's—twinkled. "You little turkey, I can't even pretend to be mad at you."

She took her fist out of her mouth long enough to coo at him.

"Yeah, I know. I can't leave you sitting in that disgusting mess. Give me a second." He laid her on the changing table and kept a hand on her stomach while he pulled out a diaper, the wipes, and baby powder. Z paused. "Now, I know last time you thought it was hilarious to make a mess all over your poor dad, but this time is going to be different. Agreed?" She cooed again, which was as good as it was going to get.

He took a deep breath and went to work, going through each step as quickly and thoroughly as he could. Five minutes later, she was cleaned, powdered, and in a new diaper, all without any explosions or traumatic events. Z disposed of the gross diaper. "There, that wasn't so bad, was it?"

It was worlds better than the first diaper change. He... didn't like to think about that, about how completely incapable the concept had made him feel. Parts of it seemed to come to Sara so naturally, while he was left a lumbering fool. But he'd learned, and when Sara got overwhelmed or exhausted past the point of reason, he was there to shoulder what she'd let him.

God, he loved that woman.

Z took Ivy and leaned against the doorway into the kitchen, bouncing her gently in the way she liked. "Your mama is something else, baby girl."

Sara glanced at him over her shoulder. "No trauma this time?"

"None." He ran his free hand over Ivy's dark curls. "She was a perfect angel."

Sara left the stove and walked over to press a kiss to their daughter's forehead and another to his lips. When she stepped back, her grin was damn near wicked. "So...I was thinking."

"Oh yeah?" He watched her, noting that she'd done something different with her hair today. He'd missed it earlier.

"Yeah." Her grin widened. "Once Ivy is asleep, I want you."

It took a full two breaths for her meaning to penetrate. "You mean—"

"Yep."

They hadn't been intimate since Ivy. She'd gotten the okay from her doctor last month, but babies didn't leave a lot of energy left over for that kind of thing. He wouldn't lie and say he hadn't spent many long showers working off energy, but Z also cherished the fact he was able to spend his nights in Sara's bed, with her body fitting perfectly against him. He hadn't said a damn thing about sex, because he refused to pressure her before she was ready.

Apparently she was ready.

"You don't have to."

Sara rolled her eyes. "Yeah, I know. I want to. God, you have no idea how much I want to."

Suddenly their daughter's bedtime couldn't come soon enough.

All through dinner, Z's focus narrowed on Sara. Yeah, he played with Ivy and did the dishes and the other little things that had built up while he was gone during the day, but he was painfully aware of every move she made. Time seemed to pass quickly and nowhere near quickly enough.

He had a beer on the couch while Sara disappeared into Ivy's room, sipping it slowly while the television droned in the background. Already, he was rock hard and aching, but he wasn't going to tackle her the second she came through that door.

No, he wanted to make this special for her.

Z leaped to his feet and headed into the bedroom. It took ten minutes to get everything set up. He finished lighting the candles as the door opened and she stepped into the room. The delight on her face made it all worth it and more. "Oh, Z."

He looked around the room, trying to see it as she did. He'd lit a dozen candles on the dresser and nightstands, leaving the bed bathed in soft light. It wasn't much, but from her expression it was more than enough. "Come here, sweetheart."

She stepped into his arms and went up onto her tiptoes to kiss him. "I love you."

"I love you, too." He lost himself in the feel of her in his arms, her body soft against his, her hips moving in a demanding way that he was all too eager to satisfy. But first he had one last question. "Hard or soft?" Tonight was about her, which meant he needed to know.

He felt her smile against his mouth. "I have to choose?"

Well, fuck. He shuddered, determined to keep himself under control. "No, sweetheart. You don't have to choose." He laid her down on the bed and set about stripping her. Though he'd seen her naked countless times in the last year, it felt new and different this time. Z spent long minutes worshipping her breasts, before kissing his way down her stomach. Her cry when he dragged his tongue over her clit was music to his ears. He took his time, driving her closer and closer to the edge, relishing every sound she made and every time her hips lifted to meet him.

Sara came with a cry, and he wasted no time moving up her body to settle between her legs. Z entered her, inch by inch, gauging her reactions every step of the way. She dug her heels into the mattress, trying to take him deeper, but he stopped her with a hand on her hip. "I'm trying not to hurt you."

"Let me worry about that. I *need* you." She hitched a leg over his hip and sighed when he gave in and sheathed his cock completely inside her. "Oh God, yes."

He kissed her, moving in her until he wasn't sure where he stopped and she began. He took the angle she loved so much—the one guaranteed to drive her out of her mind over and over again—needing to feel her come around his cock. "Come for me, sweetheart. I want to feel you."

"So…demanding."

"Yes." He bit the sensitive spot where her neck met her shoulder, and that was all it took to send her hurtling over the edge. He tried to hold back, tried to keep control, but it was too much. Z pounded into her once, twice, a third time, and came hard enough to make him see stars. He rolled to the side, keeping her tucked against his chest.

"Damn, I missed that."

"Me, too." He brushed her hair back from her face. "But I'd happily never have sex again if it means I get you and Ivy in my life."

She laughed softly. "Luckily, it's not an either-or situation. You get us and you get hot sex, too."

"Lucky me."

A strange look crossed her face. Almost nervous. "Lucky both of us."

He frowned. "What's wrong? Damn it, I *did* hurt you, didn't I?"

"What? No. No, it's nothing like that." She cuddled closer, the tension in her body giving lie to her words.

He took a deep breath, trying to get enough emotional distance to approach this in the right way. Sara had proven time and again that a direct confrontation made her dig in her heels. He took another breath. "Please tell me what's wrong."

"Z…" She lifted her head. "I love you more than I ever thought possible, and the last year has been insane and wonderful and a roller coaster that I don't want to get off of. And you've been there every step of the way." Her smile was soft and sweet. "You asked me a question back then—multiple times."

He swore to God that his heart skipped a beat. She was talking about his proposing. "I did."

"I said no—more than once." Her smile trembled a little. "I'd like to change that answer. So, Zebadiah Loreto, would you do me the honor of being my husband and making an honest woman of me?"

Joy threatened to turn him mute, but he soldiered past

it and gathered her close. "Fuck, yes. I'd marry you right this goddamn second if there was a priest around."

She laughed. "As much as I share the sentiment, I think I'd like the whole nine yards. The big dress, the tiered cake, a church packed with our friends and family."

It was all too easy to imagine standing at the altar and watching her walk down the aisle toward him, a vision in white. Z kissed her. "Anything, sweetheart. If you want me to go catch a flock of fucking doves with my bare hands to release that day, I'll do it."

"I'll remember you said that." They both tensed when Ivy's cry cut through the wall between their rooms. Sara dropped her head onto his chest. "In the meantime, reality intrudes."

"I got her." He climbed out of bed and pulled on a pair of sweats. Z paused at the door and turned to look at her. "You just made me the happiest man alive, Sara Reaver."

"Good." She stretched, her body a long line he wanted to spend a few more hours worshipping. "Remember that the next time you're changing a poopy diaper." Her laughter followed him from the room, a perfect match for his own.

Acknowledgments

To God – For a year with more ups than downs.

To Heather Howland – For helping polish up this book until it shines.

To Kari Olson – For your input on the story and for always being ready with inspirational pictures. Someone has to answer the hard questions, and you're always there to laugh no matter how outrageous my commentary is.

To PJ Schnyder and Seleste DeLaney – For always being there to chat, bounce ideas off of, and basically be a wonderful support system.

To Tim – For your unrelenting support and respect, even when this job makes me batty. I love you like a love song.

To the Rabble Rousers – For your support and excitement for each new book. You guys are amazing!

And last, but certainly not least, to all my readers – I couldn't do this without you. I am constantly humbled and amazed by you. Thank you so much!

About the Author

New York Times and USA Today bestselling author, Katee Robert, learned to tell stories at her grandpa's knee. Her favorites then were the rather epic adventures of The Three Bears, but at age twelve she discovered romance novels and never looked back. Though she dabbled in writing, life got in the way, as it often does, and she spent a few years traveling, living in both Philadelphia and Germany. In between traveling and raising her two wee ones, she had the crazy idea that she'd like to write a book and try to get published.

Explore the Serve miniseries...

OWNED BY FATE

Journalist Caroline Preston arrives at Serve, the city's hottest BDSM club, with one goal—to hate it. But then she sees him. Ripped. Rough. Eyes that could incinerate a girl's panties. As the owner of the club, Jonah Briggs sole purpose is to ensure that his clientele get everything they need, but when he sees Caroline, his only thought is what he wants—to give the sexy little reporter the most exquisite pleasure she's ever experienced...if she'll let him.

EXPOSED BY FATE

When Eliza Ballas attends New York's premier BDSM club, she's taken aback by the sexy Brit who assumes she's adept at sensual arts. She needs an erotic education fast, and she knows just the man to teach her. Oliver Preston never turns from pleasure, but Eliza's his sister's best friend. Torn between a sense of duty and his need to make her his, he draws Eliza deep into his world of exquisite pleasure, knowing he'll have to give her to another man...if he doesn't lose himself to her first.

MISTAKEN BY FATE

With seduction in sight, fashion designer Ridley Ethridge arranges to meet her potential Mr. Almost Perfect anonymously at a club that caters to erotic appetites. What happens next is both intense and satisfying—until Ridley's blindfold comes off to reveal the twin brother of Mr. Almost Perfect. The same twin who broke her heart eight years ago before he enlisted. Garrett Reaver will be damned before he lets someone else have Ridley. They have some seriously unfinished business to take care of...and it starts now.

Betting on Fate

Penelope Carson loves to steal clients from Will Reaver. Her business nemesis is the living embodiment of a controlled, powerful Norse god. Which she should have remembered before she made a bet with him, because losing means becoming Will's personal submissive for a week. There's nothing Will would like more than to have Penelope kneeling before him in complicit submission. But their bet takes them deeper than either has ever been, where control is an illusion and hearts become the stakes in a game that neither Dominant nor submissive can win...

Driven by Fate

Francesca "Frankie" De Luca always pays her debts. Even when it means stepping inside Serve, the sensuous Manhattan club that caters to particular adult desires. For Frankie, it's a taste of something she's always wanted, and never received. Until a sharply dressed Brit orders her into his room, and instructs her to undress before delivering the carnal punishment she so desperately needs. Then he offers Frankie a deal she can't refuse—and the only thing she owes him is submission...

Also by Katee Robert

Come Undone series

Wrong Bed, Right Guy

Chasing Mrs. Right

Two Wrongs, One Right

Seducing Mr. Right

Out of Uniform series

In Bed with Mr. Wrong

His to Keep

Seducing the Bridesmaid

Meeting His Match

Sanctify series

The High Priestess

Queen of Swords

Queen of Wands

CPSIA information can be obtained at www.ICGtesting.com
Printed in the USA
LVOW08s0401190816

500953LV00001B/8/P